The Four-Story Mistake

OTHER YEARLING BOOKS YOU WILL ENJOY:

YEARLING BOOKS/YOUNG YEARLINGS/YEARLING CLASSICS are designed especially to entertain and enlighten young people. Charles F. Reasoner, Professor Emeritus of Children's Literature and Reading, New York University, is consultant to this series.

For a complete listing of all Yearling titles, write to Dell Readers Service, P.O. Box 1045, South Holland, Illinois 60473.

THE BROOK

The Four-Story Mistake

WRITTEN AND ILLUSTRATED BY

ELIZABETH ENRIGHT

A YEARLING BOOK

Published by
Dell Publishing
a division of
The Bantam Doubleday Dell Publishing Group, Inc.
666 Fifth Avenue
New York, New York 10103

The trademark Yearling® is registered in the U.S. Patent
and Trademark Office.

ISBN: 0-440-42514-X

Reprinted by arrangement with Henry Holt & Company, Inc.

Printed in the United States of America

One Previous Edition

June 1987

10 9 8 7 6 5 4

CW

To my mother

CONTENTS

ILLUSTRATIONS

The Four-Story Mistake

CHAPTER I

The Last Time and the First

"**W**ELL, thank goodness there aren't going to be any more children here anyway!" said Randy crossly. She spoke crossly because she was sad and she preferred sounding cross to sounding sorrowful, even though there was no one in the room except herself. Nobody and nothing, for that matter: her words had the particular ringing echo that is heard only in entirely empty rooms.

Almost all her life Randy had shared this room with her older sister, Mona, and today they were going to go away and leave it. Forever. She looked carefully around because it is important to see clearly when one looks at something for the last time. How strange it seemed with all the furniture gone: smaller, somehow. In the long window the scarred shade hung crookedly as it always had; for hundreds and hundreds of nights its gentle flapping had been the last sound she heard before she slept. Good-bye, shade, thought Randy sentimentally. Above the place where her bed had been some of her own drawings remained because she had impulsively stuck them to the wallpaper with glue when she couldn't find the thumbtacks. Cuffy had given her a good scolding for that, all right! Good-bye, pictures,

3

thought Randy. She didn't mind leaving the pictures so much; she could make thousands of better ones any time she felt like it. She looked at the darker rectangles on the paper where other pictures had hung, and the stain on the baseboard where Mona had spilled the iodine that time.

Randy sighed a loud, echoing sigh. Downstairs in Rush's room she could hear the voices of Rush and Mona, and a lot of scraping and thumping and banging as they tried to get a suitcase closed. "Doggone thing acts like it hates me!" she heard Rush complain bitterly.

"Be reasonable," said Mona in her most maddening voice. "You can't expect anything to absorb seven times its own capacity. Why don't you take something out?"

"I suppose I *could* carry the Ninth Symphony, and the B Minor Concerto, and the roller skates myself. They don't seem to give much."

Randy sighed again and went out of the room for the last time. The last time: she'd been saying that to herself all day. She had paid a farewell visit to every single room in the house from the Office, which had been the Melendy children's playroom, to the furnace room in the basement. All of them looked bare and cold and friendless.

That morning the moving men had swarmed through the place, rolling up carpets, packing barrels, lumbering up and down the stairs with couches and chests of drawers on their backs like mammoth snails. Everything about the moving men was huge: their big striped aprons, their swelling necks and biceps, and their voices. Especially their voices; they had bawled at each other like giants shouting from mountaintops: "GIVE US A HAND WITH THE PIANNA, AL," or "CAREFUL OF THAT CORNER, JOE, DON'T

KNOCK THEM CASTERS OFF." But now they had gone, and all the furniture with them; swallowed up in two vans the size of two Noah's arks; and the house was an echoing shell, bereft and desolate.

Soon the painters and plasterers and carpenters would come into the house. They would patch up the ceiling, bolster up the sagging staircase, paint, and polish and mend till every sign of the Melendys was gone: the iodine stain on the baseboard, Randy's pictures, plasticene marks on the Office ceiling, the height-measuring marks of each Melendy child on the upstairs bathroom door, and all the dozens of other souvenirs left by four busy children in a home. The new people who had bought the house were old: a doctor and his wife. They were rich, too. How quiet the place would be under its new pelt of thick carpet. Old feet would go slowly up and down the stairs, doors would never slam, meals would be served on time by noiseless servants.

"Poor house," said Randy. For a minute she almost hated Father for selling their nice home without a word and buying a new one in the country that nobody but he and Cuffy had even seen.

"Randy!" bellowed Rush from downstairs. "Come sit on my suitcase with Mona and me. The darn thing won't close!"

Randy went down the stairs slowly, her hand trailing on the banister. Good-bye, stairs, she was thinking. Good-bye, banister: Fat Oliver won't be here any more to go sliding down you with his breeches whistling and his shoes rattling against the spokes. I bet that old doctor and his old wife never slid down a banister in their lives.

"Take your time, Madam Queen. We're young. We've got all our lives to wait," said Rush as Randy drifted mournfully into the room. His battle with the suitcase had made him cross. Or was it something else? None of them wanted to leave their house. None of them, that is, except seven-year-old Oliver who always greeted the future as a friend and never gave a hang about anything in the past. Oliver had said, "Oh, boy! A house in the country? Can I have a horse and a pig and a swing and a two-wheel bicycle?"

Rush's suitcase stood in the middle of his dismantled room along with another suitcase, two books of music scores, and the dog Isaac's carrier. Its jaws were wide open, disclosing an undigested meal of socks, underwear, field glasses, baseball mitts, sweaters, model airplanes, and books. Mona was kneeling beside it, her fair hair tousled and her cheeks crimson with exertion.

"That suitcase looks as if it were laughing out loud," Randy said.

"Oh, stop being whimsical," snapped Rush. "Come on and *sit* on it!"

So they all sat down and made their sitting as heavy as they could, and Rush struggled with the clasps which still wouldn't quite close.

"You'll just have to take out something else," sighed Mona.

"No, I won't!" Rush stood up angrily. "I'm not going to be conquered by a third-rate piece of luggage. I'll get Cuffy! Why didn't I think of it before?" and he leaned over the banister and shouted for Cuffy, who was the Melendy housekeeper, nurse, cook, adviser, and dear friend. She was the sort of person who could have been set down in the middle of the Gobi Desert and still contrived to make a homelike atmosphere about her.

"All right. All *right*," answered her voice from downstairs in the kitchen. "I'm just getting Oliver's face washed. I'll be up in a minute."

Rush came back into the room and stood silent at the window looking down into the street below. Randy and Mona sat side by side on the suitcase and looked at the bare floor. Nobody said anything.

Randy could feel the house around her, and how tall and deep and still it was. She could feel the emptiness of every room like an ache in her bones. Tonight when they were gone there would be nothing left in the house: the old boards would stretch and creak a little, the Office mouse would come out of his hiding place fearlessly, and lights from cars passing in the street would move across the ceilings of deserted rooms.

"I don't *want* to go away!" Randy burst out rebelliously. "I'll never like any house as much as this one. I don't care if it has a real swimming pool and gold doorknobs!"

"Oh, quit it, Randy." Rush turned from his window. "None of us want to move. But we have to."

Mona put her arm around Randy's shoulders. "I know how you feel," she said. "But maybe we'll like this new place, too."

"*I* won't," declared Randy, closing her eyes and holding her breath so that the tears would go back where they belonged, and not pour out and disgrace her.

Cuffy came creaking up the stairs and Oliver clumped behind her.

"Now what's the matter?" she asked breathlessly, one hand against her side. "My lands, I'm glad the new house don't have all them stairs."

"But it'll have some stairs won't it, Cuffy? And it'll have a swing, won't it? And a room for me all by myself?" pleaded Oliver, trotting beside her.

"Just sit down on my suitcase will you, Cuff?" said Rush. "It won't shut."

Cuffy had a kind heart, a good temper, an elastic patience, and she weighed closer to two hundred pounds than she cared to admit. When she sat down beside Mona on the suitcase, Randy fell off; there was no room for her. The suitcase gave a sort of leathery groan and closed. Rush sprang forward and snapped the catches as if he were trapping a lion.

"There's two advantages to being stout," Cuffy said. "One, you can shut suitcases with your weight alone and, two, it takes a lot to sweep you off your feet. Here, Rush, Mona, give me a hand and help me up. It takes a lot to get you on your feet, too," she added regretfully. "*Oliver!* I just *washed* your face! However did you get it dirty again?"

Oliver looked at her innocently. There was a lop-sided beard of dust on his chin, and two dark stripes on his forehead.

"Me? *I* don't know, Cuffy. I didn't do anything."

"He could stand in the middle of a clinic and get dirt on him," Rush said. "He exerts a magnetic action which attracts soot, dust, egg stain, chalk marks, strawberry jam, and ink."

"Look who's talking!" jeered Mona. "It's only about the

last year, Rush, that Cuffy hasn't had to send you back to wash your neck *every single time!*"

"Hullo, there!" called a voice from downstairs in the kitchen. "Anybody home?"

"Oh, it's Willy," Cuffy said. "Up here, Willy. Please help us with the luggage."

Willy Sloper had been the Melendys' furnace man for as long as any of the children could remember; and now he was coming to the country with them.

"From furnace man to farm hand in one quick change," Willy had said. "Don't know how it's gointa work out. Only livestock I ever handled was dray hosses and alley cats. Only poultry I'm acquainted with is sparras and pigeons. Only garden I ever grew was on a fire escape. Only diggin' I ever done was in the furnace to get the ashcs, or on the front stoop to clear thc snow. But we'll see—"

"Why, Willy, how grand you look!" said Mona. They all stared at Willy, who was wearing a brown felt hat which he forgot to remove, an overcoat, and long taffy-colored shoes. They had never seen him before except in his old blue jeans, patched sweater, furnace man's shoes, and cap with the ear flaps down. They hardly knew him. He picked up the two suitcases and carried them down to the front hall where the rest of the luggage was waiting in a patient herd. Rush followed with the scores and Isaac's carrier. But where was Isaac? The search for him lasted nearly ten minutes and then he was found shivering miserably under the basement washtub.

"Poor dog, he doesn't want to leave, either," said Randy dolefully.

"Aw, he doesn't care where he goes," said Rush, in his toughest manner. "All he's thinking about is how much he hates his carrier."

Willy Sloper got a taxicab. The luggage was bundled into it and strapped onto it until it looked less like a taxi than a moving van. Randy put on her old brown hat with the elastic that was so tight under the chin she couldn't swallow. Oliver had a last trace of soot removed from his face with a damp handkerchief, and Mona hid behind a door and put some powder on her nose.

"Come, my lambs," said Cuffy. "We haven't much time to spare."

All of them looked back as they went out the door, except Rush and Oliver. Rush because he wouldn't, and Oliver because it simply didn't occur to him. Behind them the front door closed. For the last time, Randy thought again. It had a hollow sound as it closed on all that emptiness.

Somehow they fitted themselves into the taxi, but there was little room for free movement afterward. "My nose itches, Cuffy," Oliver complained. "But I can't get my hand up to scratch it."

As they drove away Randy managed to turn her head and look back. The elastic of her hat bit cruelly into her neck, but she caught a last glimpse of the house. It seemed as if the house looked back at her helplessly with all its empty windows.

The train ride to the country was not very interesting. Rain blurred the glass so that it was hard to see out; Isaac howled and wailed, to the annoyance of the other passengers and the hot embarrassment of Rush; and Oliver got sick from excitement. He sat very still, looking blue around the mouth, and answering questions with short, cautious answers. Randy and Mona sat opposite him and Cuffy, while Rush (with Isaac's carrier on his lap) sat beside Willy Sloper like a man of the world and discussed Major League baseball when he could make himself heard above Isaac.

A diversion was caused by the sudden loud, clear ringing of the alarm clock in Cuffy's suitcase. The suitcase was on the rack overhead under two hatboxes and a raincoat, so they just had to sit and listen until it ran down. The noise caused Isaac to burst into even more ambitious yelps of protest; and the other passengers stared at the Melendys as if they were a family of typhoid carriers.

"Oliver, did you set that clock?" hissed Cuffy.

"I guess maybe I did," admitted Oliver guiltily. He was in the habit of setting the alarms on all the clocks he came in contact with for the sheer simple pleasure he derived from hearing them go off. But this was something he hadn't bargained for. It jarred the stomach-ache right out of him. After that he spent a very happy hour and a half traveling back and forth from the water cooler with paper cups full of water.

Finally when it was beginning to get dark the conductor marched through the car shouting "BRAX-TON. BRAX-ton. Braxton next stop!" And the Melendys went through their usual scramble of getting themselves assembled.

"I see Father! I see Father!" shrieked Oliver ecstatically as the train stopped, and in the next moment they were all hurling themselves upon their highly valued, only parent.

"Where is the house? Where is it?" cried Oliver, looking about him as if he had expected Father to bring it to the station.

"Miles away," said Father. "Right out in the country. In a valley."

In a valley. That sounded promising; Randy took her place in the taxi. It was much bigger than city taxis and she had room to turn comfortably and look out through the rain-spangled window at the streets of the town. The maple trees were yellow but most of the others were still green; set back among leaves she saw the houses, neat and respectable looking, each with its lawn. She saw two boys in slickers, and a wet horse pulling a wagon, and a cat on a front porch, and dozens of beds of soaked chrysanthemums bowing heavily under the rain and wind.

By and by there were no more houses: only green, and trees and telegraph poles rising up, one after the other, and sweeping by in a dignified dance. The road stretched ahead of them blue-grey and shining, like the back of a whale. They traveled along it and traveled along it. Oliver nodded with sleep on Cuffy's lap. Then the taxi slowed, turned in at a wide gate, and bumped along a dirt road. The trees tossed under the wind and leaves flew through the air and clung damply to the windshield.

"This is the beginning of it," Father said, and even Oliver roused himself expectantly. The car went up a hill with woods on each side, and then down again to a valley, and there was the house! It was white and square, with a mansard roof and a cupola on top. It seemed too broad for its height, and the cupola sitting in the middle of the roof looked like a foolish little hat. The children liked the way it looked. Two huge black trees grew beside the house, and lots of other trees, and behind it the woods rose steeply: they glowed with the wild luminous green of a rainy twilight. Randy's heart lifted hopefully in spite of her.

The taxi stopped and Father got out. He stood there in the rain, flourishing his hat, and said, "Welcome to the Four-Story Mistake!"

"The *what?*" cried everyone; and the taxi driver helped himself to a hearty laugh.

"The Four-Story Mistake," Father repeated.

"But it hasn't *got* four stories," Mona objected. "Unless you count the little tower on top."

"That's just the point," Father said. "This was built in 1871 by a very rich gentleman named Cassidy who had a wife and fourteen children. They took up a lot of room, as you can imagine, so when he bought this piece of land he commissioned an architect to build him a four-story house. Then he took his family to Europe for the Grand Tour, leaving the house to get itself built in his absence. The Cassidys were gone two years, and when they returned they found only a *three-*story house awaiting them. Nobody knows whose fault it was. But poor Mr. Cassidy was less rich on his return than he'd been before and he couldn't afford to have the fourth story added; the best he could do was to build that little cupola to try and give the house more height, and they just squeezed into it somehow, and ever since it's been known as the Four-Story Mistake."

"Let's hope it doesn't turn out to be a mistake to live in," said Rush. Then they all wiped their feet on the door-mat, because Cuffy reminded them, and went into the house. They sniffed the new smell of it like a pack of young hounds. It smelled of mustiness and fresh paint and wood smoke: rather pleasant, but not yet the smell of home. It looked all right, too, though the furniture hadn't settled down in its new surroundings. Half a dozen chairs clustered together like people after church, the couch was full of books, and on the marble-topped table Father's statue of the goddess Kuan Yin stood serenely beside the typewriter, a large tin of floor-wax, and a pair of tennis shoes.

"Where's my piano?" demanded Rush. "Where are my photographs?" demanded Mona. "Am I really going to have a room all by myself?" asked Oliver. "Are there owls in the woods?" asked Randy. Isaac ran madly from room to room uttering short barks, Cuffy clashed among the pans in the kitchen, and Father and Willy started upstairs with the luggage.

"Mr. Melendy," said Cuffy, reappearing in the living room, her face grave and her tone solemn, "I can't find a *thing to eat* in the kitchen!"

"Oh, Lord!" said Father helplessly, his arms pulled down by suitcases. "I guess I forgot to get anything. I was so busy getting the furniture placed that I never even thought about food!"

The children's faces fell.

"I'll drive to town and buy something," offered Willy.

"No transportation," groaned Father. "Mrs. Oliphant's lending us her station wagon but it won't get here till Thursday. The nearest village is three miles away, and it's raining pitchforks."

"Can't we phone, then?"

"Phone's not in yet," said Father unhappily. "The man said he'd come today, but of course he didn't."

But Cuffy decided that Mr. Melendy had been punished enough.

"Well, I brought some odds and ends along in one of my bags," she said. "Leftovers from the kitchen. Didn't want to leave 'em for them new people! Maybe I can throw something together."

Father and Willy proceeded up the stairs relieved, and the children followed at their heels. The house was so big that there was a bedroom for each of them and even one left over in case they had a guest. They ran about exploring one another's rooms. "Look, mine has a *window* seat" shouted Randy; and then feeling that she was being disloyal to their last house, she added, "But I liked the wallpaper in my old one best."

Mona said, "Mine has a little alcove and I'm going to make a dressing table to fit into it. A real one with a ruffle, and a powder box on it that plays music."

Rush said, "Mine has a tree outside it that I think I can climb down."

Oliver said, "Mine is for me all by myself and nobody else." He had always slept in the same room with Cuffy before.

And Father said, "*Mine* is down at the end of the corridor, and quiet as the tomb." He sounded very happy about that.

Then Cuffy called them and they all went down to the kitchen and had a strange, interesting supper of shredded wheat with brown sugar and condensed milk on it, hot cocoa, canned peaches, and cookies that tasted of card-board box.

The kitchen was bigger and higher than the one at home and the stove had a sort of black metal canopy over it, very royal. Out of doors the wind howled and the rain lashed, and right in the middle of supper the lights went out!

It was wonderful; the children loved it. "Blackout! Take cover, men! The Messerschmitts are overhead!" hissed Rush dramatically.

"Guess a wire's blew down somewheres," said Willy's voice.

"That's right. I wonder if it often happens in storms out here?" said Father. "Come on, Willy, there are some candles in a box in the front room. Help me find them, will you?"

In springing to obey Willy fell over a packing case and smashed two jelly glasses and the kitchen teapot.

"Nobody move," Cuffy ordered the children like a policeman. "I don't want nobody getting cut on glass. Soon's we have a light I'll clean it up."

They all sat in the dark and went on with their supper.

"It's interesting eating in the dark," Randy remarked. "Things taste different. They taste more."

Oliver just sat quiet with his plate in his lap. It was dark, it was strange: there they all were together inside the fortress. Outside in the enemy night the foe pressed toward the house: Nazis, Iroquois Indians, pirates, robbers, it didn't matter which. All four probably. When they got too real he put out a cautious hand, and sure enough there was Cuffy beside him. The enemy sank back affrighted.

Father and Willy reappeared with lighted candles in their hands. They were like naturalists returning with rare orchids from the jungle; there was a quiet pride about them. At that very instant the lights came on again!

"Have you ever noticed how the sun comes out if you carry an umbrella on a cloudy day?" said Father.

After supper they all had baths in the two new bathrooms. They all brushed their teeth over the new basins. Each said good night and padded into his new paint-smelling bedroom.

Randy lay in her own old bed that she was used to. It was still raining: she could hear it, and there were drops on the window. A light came and went, came and went, among the tossing branches: from Willy Sloper's room above the stable, perhaps. Maybe it was going to be nice living in the country after all. Delightful facts and probabilities floated in confusion through her mind: in bad storms the lights went out; there were woods to explore; her room had a window seat, a real window seat, where she could curl up and read, just like a girl in a bookplate. And there was a stable; maybe they could find something alive to keep in it; maybe there were hickory nut trees, she thought she smelled them; maybe there was a brook, she thought she heard one. And on top of the house there was a cupola, a tiny turret with four long windows looking east and north and west and south. Tomorrow she would explore it all for the first time. "The first time, the first time," was the refrain that sang through Randy's thoughts tonight instead of "the last time, the last time," as it had been this afternoon.

Wind and rain lapped the house in a deep ocean of

sound and movement. Glass rattled in the windows, and someplace faraway something banged from time to time: a shutter probably. Cuffy, hollow-cheeked without her teeth, tiptoed from room to room adjusting windows and pulling blankets up under chins. At last every light was out, every room was still. The house was full of sleep.

It was beginning to be home.

CHAPTER II

A View Apiece

RUSH woke up early the next morning. The bluejays woke him up. He, who could sleep through the metallic thundering of ash cans and the honking of taxis, was startled out of sleep by the jeering mew of the bluejays in the Norway spruce outside his window.

The room was strange in the daylight. There was a carved marble mantel over the fireplace with a cherub's head in the middle that looked like Henry the Eighth as a baby. But on top of the mantel were some of his books, his clock, the socks he had taken off last night, and the World's Fair savings bank with nothing in it but two aspirins, which he had dropped in there once when he was sick and was supposed to take them and didn't. And there was the little brown photograph of his mother. The sight of these possessions made him feel at home, and so did Isaac at the foot of the bed.

Rush got up and Isaac hopped down, and they both went over to the window to look out.

At first they couldn't see anything but the tangled needles of the Norway spruce beside the window. The rain had stopped hours ago, but now a heavy mist rose up from the earth and obscured the valley. After a while, as Rush watched, a tree swam into view, looking pale and ghostly; then another and another. The mist was lifting, and it was going to be a good day. The air was full of a sound of dripping, and the cries of jays, and another sound: a rushing, pouring one.

"Gosh, I believe it's a brook!" exclaimed Rush. "Why didn't Father say there was a brook? Come on, Isaac, let's go see."

With more stealth than necessary, Rush peered out into the empty hall, closed the door noiselessly behind him, and tiptoed down the stairs. A warm, hopeful smell of coffee seeped out of the kitchen. That meant that Cuffy was up already.

"Pretend it's the headquarters of a German general," Rush whispered to Isaac. "His orderly is making coffee. We've been concealed in the rafters all night, intercepting code messages. To be discovered means certain death." Crouched like an Indian, silent as a panther, Rush reached the big front door and opened it. He and Isaac stepped out, free men.

The air was moist and mild. Veils and plumes of mist drifted by like the finest smoke. Wet drops fell on Rush's head, and cold wet leaves clung to the soles of his bare feet. He couldn't stop smelling the air in great, deep, loud sniffs. It was so delicious: it smelled of water, and mud, and maple trees, and autumn.

Isaac found smells to his own taste, too: a fragrance of squirrels, and field mice, and moles, with a faint intoxicating hint of skunk. He trotted to and fro, zigzagging from side to side, doubling back, snuffing and pausing with his tail quivering, and twigs caught in his ear-fringes.

Rush walked in the direction of the roaring sound, but from time to time he found it necessary to stop and examine some new object of interest. There was a summer-house, for one thing, with cast-iron trellis walls, and a half-rotted floor full of leaves. And there was a sycamore tree with a cave in its trunk more than big enough for Rush and Isaac. A good place to come and think in. There were also two iron deer who looked as though they had been frozen in a mood of disapproval.

The roaring grew louder and louder. And then between lifting mist veils Rush saw the brook! At one point it was a broad, brown stream gliding smoothly in its course, and at the next it had turned into a little torrent brawling and hustling down between the rocks in a cascade, and breaking below into snowy eddies and cuffs of foam.

Rush stood at the edge of the little cataract, and watched it. A very valuable thing to have right in your own back yard; he felt extremely proud of it. Then he walked to the point above it where the water was held in a clear, brimming brown pool. At the bottom he could see the turning sand like brown sugar, lacy filaments of leaves, twigs with rotted bark, and stones with moss on them.

He dipped his right big toe into the pool and the cold spread upward through his leg in a little electric shock. After a moment of consideration he pulled off his pajamas and plunged in.

Cold! It was cold enough to make his teeth rattle in their sockets and his hair stand on end, and it wasn't more than three feet deep at its deepest point, but at that moment

Rush wouldn't have traded it for the pearl-lined pool of a maharaja.

"Come on, sissy," he said to Isaac, and Isaac with a look of loathing, but obedient to the last, flung himself into the water.

When Rush came out he was red as a boiled lobster and he felt like Superman. He thumped himself on the chest, and uttered several ear-splitting sounds which he fondly imagined to be good imitations of Tarzan's jungle cry. There was nothing to dry himself with except the top of his pajamas, so he used that: first on himself, and then on Isaac. Then clad only in the pajama trousers, and holding the jacket over his head like a drenched banner he marched back toward the house.

But he felt so fine with the wind tickling his bare ribs that when he came to the house he walked right past it toward the stable. He might as well see everything, he thought.

"Hi there, Robinson Crusoe, where's your clo'es?" said a voice. And Rush saw Willy Sloper sitting on an overturned bucket under a tree. There was a little fire in front of him and he was cooking something over it. Something that smelled equally delicious to both Rush and Isaac with their differently attuned noses.

"Hi, Willy. What's cooking?"

"My breakfast," Willy said. "Coffee. Hot, black coffee, strong enough to lift a safe. And bacon; crisp, juicy bacon. And eggs still warm from the grocery store. I done the marketin' early; I rode to the village with the milkman and I rode back with the garbage collector. Awful nice fellas both of 'em. Want some breakfast?"

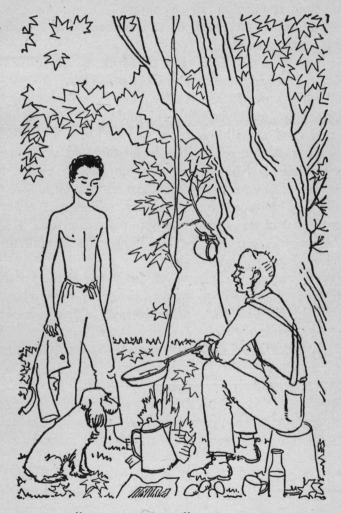

"MY BREAKFAST," WILLY SAID

Rush refused politely although he could feel the hunger in his stomach uncoiling like a cobra.

"Why don't you go up to the kitchen, Willy? Cuffy will give you breakfast."

"I know, I know. But it's just that I like eating outdoors this way. It reminds me of Van Cortlandt Park."

"It's the gypsy in you," Rush said.

"The hobo, more likely," Willy told him. "I always had a kinda good-for-nothing streak in me, like a stray dog. I always kinda thought I'd like to hit the road; walk, and ride the rails, and be a bum. Carry my coffee pot on a string around my neck; and not have nothing on my back in the way of responsibilities except a change of clo'es, an extry pair of shoes, and this here old frying pan."

"Why didn't you ever?" asked Rush, who thought the idea sounded pretty good himself.

"Well, I tellya. It's from my father's side of the family I get this idea 'bout hittin' the road. But from my mother's side of the family I get a mean conscience that's always kep' me earnin' my livin' whether I wanted to or not."

Willy sighed, and removed bacon from the frying pan to a thick chipped plate.

"Ain'tcha cold? Whereya been?"

"Swimming," said Rush dreamily, watching Willy break four eggs into the frying pan and set them over the fire.

"Swimming! That you I heard a while back makin' them noises?"

"Yes, I was being Tarzan," Rush explained.

"Tarzan! Sounded more to me like a rooster with the croup!"

Rush didn't reply. He was staring fascinated at the eggs.

He watched the transparent whites become opaque, changing from liquid to solid. He watched their four golden eyes looking up at him enticingly. He swallowed, unable to stir or to remove his gaze from those hypnotic eggs.

"Want some?" said Willy.

"Oh, no, thanks, Willy," said Rush faintly. "My own breakfast will be ready in a few minutes."

"Aw, come on," said Willy, and gave him an enormous plateful. "Want some coffee?"

"Well-uh. I never had any. I mean black like that."

"Oh, it won't hurt ya. I drank black coffee when I was eight years old. Time I was your age I chewed tobacca. Never hurt me none."

Rush took the hot tin cup in his hands. The first swallow was so hot he could feel wrinkles on his tongue after he had taken it. And the black bitter taste of it didn't please him much, but he couldn't be less of a man at thirteen than Willy had been at eight, so he drank two cups, smacking his lips.

"Next time I'll teach ya to chew," Willy called as Rush reeled dizzily back to the house.

"Rush *Melendy!*" said Cuffy. "Why are you only wearing your pajama pants? Don't you know this is the middle of October?"

"I've been swimming," Rush explained.

"*Swimming!*" said Cuffy outraged; and "*Swimming,*" said Randy incredulously as she came into the kitchen, "swimming in *what?*"

"There's a brook," Rush said. "I discovered it. We've got a brook on our property."

Randy started for the door, but Cuffy caught her by her overall straps.

"No, you don't, my duck. Not till you've eaten every bit of breakfast. Here, Rush, here's your sweater. Put it on and eat your breakfast while it's hot. You can dress later."

There was no help for it. Rush had to sit down and eat breakfast all over again: every mouthful. Oatmeal and eggs and bacon and toast and milk. Cuffy watched him like an eagle at meals nowadays, because she thought he was too thin. Rush chewed until his jaws ached and his eyes watered; he might as well have been eating sawdust. But at last it was over, and he started up the stairs, moving slowly and heavily; weighted down with breakfast.

He met Mona on the stairs.

"For goodness' sake, Rush," she said. "Why do you look so funny?"

"Born that way," Rush replied glumly.

"No, I mean why are you holding your stomach? Have you got a pain?"

Rush paused wearily, like an actor playing Hamlet. "Mona," he said, "it might interest you to know that I'm carrying a heavy burden. For breakfast today I was forced by circumstance to consume four eggs: two fried, two boiled. Also nine pieces of bacon. Nine. Also one bowl of oatmeal, man-size. Also one piece of toast as big as a barn door, with marmalade on it. Also one glass of milk, and two large cups of black coffee. Now do you understand?"

"What is it, a contest or something? *Coffee!* You mean Cuffy let you?"

"Sh. No, silly. Today I attended two breakfasts. At

Willy's coffee was served. Then in order to avoid complications I ate a second one at Cuffy's request."

"How revolting," said Mona, continuing downstairs. It had been her favorite word for some time now.

After everyone had had breakfast, and every dish was washed and every bed made, Father took them up to the third floor to see the new Office.

"I'm going to let you do the organizing and arranging yourselves," he told them. "I had the carpenter put up some shelves, and the moving men dumped the furniture anywhere. It's up to you, now."

The room was really an attic, large, oblong, with deep dormer windows on three sides, and a drum-shaped coal stove attached to the brick chimney mass by a round black pipe. The old carpet lay in a long roll, and in the middle of the bare floor the familiar Office furniture was lumped together in a huddle: the sofa with busted springs, the battered rocking horse, the blackboard, the ancient chairs, the boxes of books. In the midst of the confusion stood Rush's piano, tall and dignified, like Florence Nightingale among the wounded.

"Why, look at the walls!" cried Oliver. "There's pictures and writing all over them!"

It was true. From the ceiling to the floor the sloping walls were covered with pages of pictures and stories cut out of old papers and magazines. They were yellowish brown with age, and here and there were dark stains where the rain had leaked in, but on the whole they were remarkably well preserved, for at the tops of some of the pages there were dates. April 17, 1881, said one of them. September 19, 1879, said another.

"Look, here's a whole story pasted up; illustrations and everything. Pretty nifty, too," said Rush. "It's called 'Pursued by Siberian Wolves!' Oh, boy, look at that; a whole sleighful of men, all wearing mustaches and fur hats, and the wolves right behind with their tongues hanging out!"

"Here's another," said Mona. "Only it's called 'Dimple Sunshine and the Bad Buttercup.' You should see the picture of Dimple Sunshine: she looks about four years old but I think she's wearing a corset. High button shoes, too. How revolting. Imagine."

"There's a very int'resting one down here," piped Oliver, who was just learning to read. "It has good pictures, and it's called 'Tribble Customs in the Sudden.' What does that mean?"

"Tribble Customs in the—Here let me see," Rush bent down beside Oliver. "Oh, I get it. 'Tribal Customs in the Sudan.'"

"Well, when I was hunting for a house in the country I knew I'd have to find one that had an Office as good as the one at home," Father was saying. "When I saw this I was satisfied."

"It's swell," agreed Rush and Mona in a single voice. As for Oliver, he had practically forgotten the other house already. But Randy was silent, torn between enthusiasm for this new Office and homesick loyalty for the old one.

"Look, Randy," Father said. "See those little stairs? They go up to the cupola. Let's explore it, shall we?"

Rush had climbed over the furniture and reached his beloved piano: now he had the lid up, and standing before it he plunged into the Brahms Rhapsody he had been learning. He played it much too loud and much too fast on purpose because he was happy. It sounded like a team of runaway fire horses. Mona and Oliver were sitting side by side on the floor studying the "Tribble Customs," so Randy was the first of the children to see the cupola. She followed her father up the steep, narrow steps. Almost as good as a ladder, she thought to herself. At the top Father opened the door and there they were, standing in a tiny room that seemed to be nothing but windows. The tower of the enchanted princess, Randy thought. All around is nothing but sea. Once a day a slave in a rowboat comes bringing a basket of food. The princess pulls it up on a long silken cord. She also catches fish from the window. She—but Father was speaking.

"Poor Mr. Cassidy," he was saying. "This cupola is another part of the mistake. You see, a cupola is supposed to be built in a place which commands a splendid view: something impressive like a city in the distance, or an ocean, or a chain of mountains. Look, toward the east all you can see is the brook and the woods on the hill. Toward the west all you can see is the road winding back over another hill, through more woods. Toward the south all you can see is spruce branches and the weather vane on the stable roof. But toward the north, yes, there is a view. The only long one."

Yes, there was. Randy looked out the north window, and far, far away up the valley, which was shallow and wide; dotted with trees, and crossed with stone fences, and seamed with the brown brook that was partly theirs. At the very end of the valley she thought she saw a village: rooftops, and white walls, and smoke coming up blue into the autumn air.

"That's Carthage, three miles away," Father told her.

"There's a window for each child," Randy remarked.

"So there is," said Father, and after a minute he said, "And now that I think about it, Randy, I believe that each of these windows belongs to one of you in a particular way. This one, the north one, for instance, that looks so far up the valley. It must belong to Oliver because he's always looking ahead: always straining toward tomorrow. The east one is Rush's. The view from it is all moving and changeable: the wind stirs the trees, the water dashes and foams in the brook. And the south one. See how the dark spruce branches beyond the glass make a sort of mirror of the window. That's Mona's: she's at the age where she loves her own reflection."

"And the west window?" Randy said.

"The west window belongs to you, Randy. From it you can look back all day along the road you traveled yesterday."

Randy thought she understood what Father meant. "Well, I like today too," she said. "I like *now*. And this house. I think it's a wonderful house. Only I loved the other one, too."

"We all did," agreed Father. "But sometimes it would be nice if you and Oliver changed windows. In fact, it would be a good thing if all of you exchanged views once in a while." He gave Randy's untidy mop of curls an affectionate tug. "Well, that's over. How do you like this tower, anyway? I thought you kids might enjoy it. As a sort of retreat, you know."

"You mean it's ours?" said Randy. "Just for us children? Like part of the Office, you mean?"

"That's it," said Father.

"Oh, father, it *is* swell!" cried Randy, giving him a hug that knocked the breath out of him. "It *is* swell, and I love it. And I'll spend half an hour looking out of Oliver's window every time I come up here, just so I'll deserve it!"

CHAPTER III

Ali-Baba Oliver

THERE was no way in which the Melendy children could go to school until Mrs. Oliphant's station wagon arrived. The Carthage public school was three miles away, and though Rush liked to picture himself swinging along the country road in the morning like Abraham Lincoln, the thought of returning by the same lengthy route had less glamour. Willy's friend, Mr. Purvis, the garbage collector, said he'd be glad to take two of the children to town each morning, but there'd be no room for the other two except in back with the garbage. Oliver couldn't see why this wasn't a practical arrangement. Still they hadn't so long to wait. They had arrived on Friday evening, and the station wagon was due to appear on the following Thursday.

In the interval they unpacked, and explored, and had picnics every day in a different place. Their range seemed almost unlimited, for there were thirty acres of land that went with the house, and a sample of everything delightful, short of an active volcano and an ocean, that one could want on his own territory: brook, woods, stable, hollow tree, and summerhouse. Each of the children had found something that belonged particularly to him by right of discovery. Rush had found the brook, of course, and Mona discovered the orchard: it was full of warped old trees covered with suckers, and the apples that had fallen in the grass tasted half wild and bitter sweet. Randy found a little cave, and a swampy place where fringed gentians were in blossom, but her important discovery was to come later.

Oliver found the cellar.

Of course they all knew that there was a cellar but nobody, except Willy, had ever been down to look at it, and even he had looked at nothing but the furnace. It remained for Oliver, on the third day, to open an inconspicuous door off the kitchen and find the dusty stone steps going downward into darkness. A rank, delicious smell of cold stone and damp filled Oliver's nostrils. Prudently and quietly he closed the door; this was to be his own personal voyage of discovery, and no one was going to be allowed to assist or interfere.

He tiptoed up the back stairs to borrow Rush's flashlight, without mentioning his intention to Rush who was conveniently practicing in the Office. Then he tiptoed down again, through the kitchen, and past Cuffy's broad, preoccupied back at the stove. Once again he opened the inconspicuous door, stepped in, and closed it quietly behind him. The flashlight led him down the steps by its circle of light.

The floor of the cellar was concrete, and its walls were the stone foundations of the house. The air of the place was dank and still, like the air of a medieval dungeon; Oliver breathed it deeply. Overhead dangled a fixture with no bulb in it, but he saw that there were windows, small windows flush with the ceiling. They glowed with a filtered, greenish light, being almost entirely smothered by grass stems, weeds, and clinging tentacles of Virginia creeper. He switched off the flashlight, enjoying the mysterious gloom. A second later he switched it on again, his heart pounding in his chest, and saw that what he had taken in the dimness to be an indescribable monster was nothing but a large coal furnace. Something like the one at home only bigger and more complicated, with great brawny pipes and tubes, and a grate in its lower door that looked like teeth in an iron mouth.

"Hello, furnace," Oliver said placatingly. He opened the door with the grate and stuck his head in, and sniffed the smell of dead ashes. He turned the flashlight into it, too, but saw nothing except some very old cinders, so he closed the door and went on with his exploring. The only other things in the furnace room were a stack of dry logs that crackled from time to time as though full of mice, and a bin with coal in it. Oliver went into the bin and climbed up and down the slipping mountain of coal; he fell once or twice but that only added to his pleasure and the damage of his clothes. He pretended he was climbing a crater in the Valley of Ten Thousand Smokes. At the end of fifteen minutes, when he emerged, he was black as a Cardiff coal miner and extremely happy.

From the furnace room two other chambers opened out. In the first one Oliver found an old bedspring, an empty barrel, and a Mason jar high up on the window sill containing nothing but a large, hairy spider which he did not disturb. The spider's web was laced across the window, and was hung with dried fragments of moth wings, and the husks of beetles and houseflies.

The second room had a wooden door which was shut. Oliver had a hard time getting it open: it was stuck in its casing as though it had not been opened for a very long time. But he pushed against it with all his weight and finally it flew open and he flew into the room with it.

He could hardly believe his eyes.

This room was smaller than the other, and it was to Oliver as the cave was to Ali Baba: a storehouse full of treasure.

The first things he saw were two sleds propped up against the wall on their hind legs. They were very old, with rusted runners, and one was red, and one was blue. Names were painted on them in fancy letters. "Snow Demon," said one; and "Little Kriss Kringle," said the other. They must have belonged to the Cassidy children, thought Oliver. And then he saw the bicycle. Upstairs in the attic there were pictures of boys riding bicycles like this one. The front wheel was taller than he was, though the back wheel was small; and the saddle and handle bars soared loftily atop the front wheel. If only my legs were longer, thought Oliver impatiently, looking down at his short, fat underpinnings; this bike is much better than the kind they have nowadays; more dangerous.

Besides the bicycle and the sleds, there was an old-fashioned tin bathtub covered with rust and chipped paint of robin's-egg blue, and shaped like an armchair with a high back. And there were more Mason jars, with more spiders in them, and a doll carriage made of decaying leather, and a broken coffee grinder, and a cast-iron crib frame, and a set of big books. All the objects in the room were covered with a layer of fine, ashy, white dust. Oliver sat down on one of the books, took another on his lap, reveling in the dust, and began to look at it. It turned out to be the bound volume of a magazine called *Harper's Young People*, published in the year 1887. The book was mildewed, some of its pages were glued together by years of damp, and its green cover had been gnawed by mice, but it exuded the indescribably delicious odor of all ancient books; better still, it was full of the pictures and adventures of the children of that other world which he had already explored on the walls of the Office upstairs. A world where girls wore sashes and long hair, and boys wore long stockings and button boots, and the horses which pulled the trolley cars wore straw hats. In that world there were no automobiles, no airplanes, no streamline trains, and yet the children seemed to be almost the same kind of children there were now.

Overhead Cuffy's feet creaked to and fro across the kitchen floor boards. Outside the morning was clear and golden with Indian summer. But Oliver sat in the dim light of his cellar room; pale and happy as a mushroom in its native habitat.

Hours later his reluctant ear was pierced by the frantically repeated sound of his name. "Oliv—er! Oliv—er!" cried Cuffy, faint and faraway. He heard her feet hurry across the kitchen floor; the screen door open. "Oliver, come in for your lunch!" called Cuffy. He sat listening and when he heard her feet go out of the kitchen he rose, closed the door of the marvelous room behind him, and ran silently up the steps.

OLIVER SAT DOWN ON ONE OF THE BOOKS

When Cuffy returned to the kitchen she found Oliver there, gazing dreamily out the window.

"Great day in the morning!" she said exasperatingly. "Where in the world have you been? And how in the world did you get so dirty?"

Oliver neatly evaded this question by answering it with one of his own. "Am I dirty, Cuffy?" he asked, looking surprised.

"I never saw such dirt. Dirt all over you, and something that looks like coal dust; and what have you got dangling from your ear? I believe it's a cobweb. Come here while I wash you."

All through lunch Oliver ate without knowing that he ate at all. A baked potato, two slices of liver, and a large helping of beets (which he detested) simply disappeared from his plate into himself without conscious material assistance on his part. Inwardly he had entered once more the little room that was his discovery, his kingdom. He dwelt longingly upon the thought of the two old sleds, the bicycle, the coffee grinder (which he planned to take apart), and above all the books. Tomorrow I'll go down again, he told himself, and whenever it rains, and when Cuffy takes a nap. But I mustn't go too often. Oliver was wise for his seven years: already he knew that to overdo a thing is to destroy it. I'll keep it secret for a long, long time, he thought. He did, too; for he had great determination, and knew the secret of keeping secrets.

Also he had a kind heart. Six weeks later when Randy had to stay home from school with a toothache he took her down to the cellar and showed her his discovery. It worked better than oil of cloves: Randy forgot her toothache for more than an hour and a half, absorbed in the dusty volumes of *Harper's Young People.*

Afterward she and Oliver referred to the secret cellar room by its initials S.C.R. They referred to it ostentatiously and often, much to the outward boredom and inward consuming curiosity of both Mona and Rush, who were not enlightened until the twenty-fifth of December when Oliver showed it to them for a Christmas present.

CHAPTER IV

The Back of the Bus

HOW Randy loved the cupola! In it she seemed to be detached from the house, and the world, floating aloft on a sea of branches. An army cot, an old rocking chair, and an empty toy chest were all the furniture it contained. Someday she planned to paint the ceiling: blue, with gold stars on it, whole constellations, and a section of the Milky Way. She would have to lie on her back on a scaffolding to paint it, the way Father told her Michelangelo had lain on his back to paint the ceiling of the Sistine Chapel. Probably she would never get around to doing it, but it was an inspiring thought.

Today she was standing at her own west window watching the road. Ever since lunch she had been standing there, for this was the day when their dear friend Mrs. Oliphant was to arrive in the antique station wagon which she always called the Motor, with a capital M.

The children knew and were fond of the Motor (though it was a difficult car to love), for they had spent the previous summer at Mrs. Oliphant's house by the sea, and had ridden in it often. It was a tall, narrow vehicle fitted with regular four-paned windows that made it look like a

RANDY REMAINED AT HER POST LIKE SISTER ANNE

greenhouse on wheels, and was further distinguished by a small length of pipe sticking up from the roof chimneywise to release the evil fumes of the exhaust.

Randy remained at her post like Sister Anne, and at four o'clock was rewarded by being the first to see the Motor rattling conservatively down the drive. It would not be hurried; it was like a self-willed old mule. Nothing in creation could make it alter its pace.

"Here she comes, kids!" shouted Randy, flinging herself recklessly down the ladder steps that led to the Office. The answering thunder of descending footsteps and shouts of joy reached her from the hall stairs. Father burst out of his study; Cuffy burst out of the kitchen; the front door was hurled open and left that way. The station wagon grumbled haughtily to a stop. Mrs. Oliphant emerged and was engulfed by enthusiastic Melendy children.

She was an old, lively lady: tall, dark-browed, and adorned with many furs, many necklaces, and brooches. The whole family loved Mrs. Oliphant. She was kind, and funny, and original: she carried with her the memory of a long life starred with adventures, and you had the feeling that, old though she was, still more adventures lay ahead of her.

"Are you tired, Mrs. O?" said Father. He always called her Mrs. O.

"Not so tired as the Motor," replied Mrs. Oliphant, looking solicitously at the station wagon. "Now that I've given it to you, I don't think it's going to last very long. You must use it carefully; after all, it's very old. It may give up the ghost at any minute."

The children stared at the car with the respect due to an elder.

"But in case it *does* give up the ghost," Mrs. Oliphant said frivolously, "I have supplied the children with other means of locomotion. It would be dreadful if they were forced to miss a single minute more of school. Look in the back of the Motor."

Oliver got there first. He opened the rear door and leaned in.

"Oh, boy," he said quietly. "Two-wheelers. Four of them. Oh, boy."

Rush and Mona and Randy pushed against him, peering into the station wagon. It was true.

"Bicycles!" shouted Randy rather obviously.

"How absolutely di—*vine!*" said Mona. Next to "revolting" it was her favorite word.

All Rush could think of to say was "Gosh!" He searched around in his mind for something more eloquent, and added "Gee!"

"Mrs. O, you shouldn't have!" objected Father. "It's too much."

But she just waved him away. "You and Cuffy will have to walk, I'm afraid. But that will be good for your figures."

She put her arm through Father's and looked up at the house.

"Well, Martin," she said to Mr. Melendy, "it looks strong and comfortable, but rather broad-shouldered for its height, don't you think?"

"That's why it's called the Four-Story Mistake," Rush told her.

"*The what?*" Mrs. Oliphant stopped walking and stared at him.

"That's its name," Rush told her, and the whole thing had to be explained again.

"It's a nice story, and a nice name," Mrs. Oliphant decided. "A much better name for a house than the usual kind like Hillcrest, or Bayview, or Casa Loma, or Shangri-La!" She began to laugh as she looked at Oliver. During the whole conversation, as they moved toward the house, he had been walking backwards in front of her. Walking is not the word, however. He was hopping, fidgeting, and jumping from one foot to the other, and staring into her face with an expression of agonized pleading.

"What's the matter, Oliver?" said the old lady.

"Please, Mrs. Ollerphant, could we practice now? On the two-wheelers?" he begged.

"By all means," she agreed. "You children stay outside and practice, and we will go indoors far away from the windows, where it's safe. Remember I am not to be held responsible for any fractures or concussions!"

Rush and Mona had ridden before. In no time at all, after a few preliminary lurchings, they were speeding showily around the circle in the drive, zigzagging across the lawn between the trees, and coasting down the side of the hill.

Randy had a hard time learning. Her bicycle behaved as though it had a life of its own, doing everything to be rid of her. It bucked like a broncho, veered captiously in all the wrong directions, flung itself at trees and walls, and fell on its side in repeated swoons. Randy fell with it every time. At the end of a half hour's patient struggle, her shins were black and blue, her knee was scraped, and she was close to tears. Rush, swooping expertly by, saw her fall for the seventeenth time and took pity on her.

"Look, Ran," he said, "you get on and I'll hold the bike for you. I won't let you fall. Now, *push* down with your right foot, now with your left. That's it. You'll have it soon."

And thanks to Rush's help she did have it soon. In a very short time she found herself sailing deliriously along the drive, under her own steam. The wind whistled against her cheek, her battered knees pumped up and down, and the bicycle, its spirit almost broken, carried her smoothly; turning when she wished it to turn, stopping when she wished it to stop. I can do anything! Randy's thoughts were singing victoriously. If I can learn to ride a bicycle I can do *anything!* Learn to fly an airplane, or dance like Baronova, or draw like Botticelli. Drunk with success she tried riding without hands, the way Rush did, and immediately fell off.

Oliver fell a lot, too. But he had taken his little bicycle to the top of a small rise and wobbled down it over and over again until finally he mastered the idea of balancing himself. He was systematic and determined, and learned much faster than Randy. The only trouble was that his legs were so short he couldn't dismount properly; so he developed his own method: while the bicycle was still going he would leap clear of it, allowing it to crash to the earth, wheels still spinning. The method wasn't very good (especially for the bicycle) but the best he could manage at the moment.

"You're doing swell now, Ran," Rush called. "How about going for a real ride?"

Oliver wisely preferred to stay at home and practice, but the rest of them walked their bicycles up the drive to the top of the hill, then they got on again and started on a voyage of discovery. Randy fell off twice, once when a squirrel ran across the road and once when she came to the stone gate, but as soon as she was out on the concrete highway she was able to manage better. The road under her wheels felt smooth as satin: She was flying, skimming effortlessly like a swallow near the earth. She kept her eyes fixed sternly on the road and stayed close to the right side. Mona and Rush grew small in the distance ahead of her.

"Hey, wait for *me!*" called Randy, but the words were blown away from her. Half elated, half afraid, she spun along the highway by herself. She didn't dare look at the cars that passed her: whisht, whisht, they went in a speedy gasp, leaving a wake of wind behind them. Fences flew by her, and houses, and cows, and trees, but she didn't see any of them. The road, the bicycle, the wind, were drawing her along faster and faster, and she had the feeling that she would never be able to stop. Ahead of her Mona and Rush swerved to the right and after a little while, when Randy got there, she swerved too.

And then her heart seemed to freeze in her chest: hard and cold as a snowball.

The long main street of Carthage sloped steeply away below her. She saw the houses and stores on each side, and the people and the cars, and the steeple on the church at the foot of the hill. Where, oh, where were Rush and Mona? Save me, save me, prayed Randy as the bicycle gathered speed. She couldn't remember how to stop or put on the brake: she just held on. In a sort of dreadful calm she rocketed down the hill, expecting to die. Clear and sharp she saw an old lady and some chickens run across the street to get out of her way: she saw the Carthage traffic cop staring at her with his mouth open. He went by in a flash. She saw the broad blue back of a parked bus in front of her growing larger and larger, and more and more convincing like a close-up in the movies. Save me, murmured Randy once again before her front wheel met the back of the bus, and she flew over the handle bars head on into the license plate.

Everything was velvet-black, and deep, and still.

When she opened her eyes she was lying comfortably in the gutter looking up into the red face of the bus driver. He had his cap on the back of his head, and a pencil behind one ear, she noticed. There were a lot of other people around, too, all looking interested and solemn.

"You all right, kid?" said the bus driver. "Hurt any-place?"

"My head hurts, kind of," Randy replied dreamily. Something warm and wet ran down her cheek.

"The victim must be kept lying down," said a lady with glasses. "That's what my first-aid book says. The victim *must* be kept lying down while someone calls a doctor."

Randy sprang to her feet. "My *bike!*" she cried. "Is my bike all right?"

"The victim don't want to lay down," cackled an old man in the crowd. Everybody laughed except the lady with glasses.

"But my new *bike!*" wailed Randy.

"Your bike's okay," said the traffic cop, who had just arrived. "But you've got a bad cut on your forehead. My house's right across the street. You come on with me, and let my wife fix you up." He gave her his handkerchief to hold against her forehead and led her across the street, supporting her with his arm. Randy felt proud and delicate; a sort of heroine; the victim of an accident!

"Poor little thing," someone said.

"My, ain't she brave!" said someone else.

Now that she knew her bike was safe, Randy enjoyed it all very much.

"Hey, Ran, are you okay?" Rush came riding up, looking scared. Behind him she saw Mona's pale face.

"I guess I am," Randy replied in a weak voice, leaning against the traffic cop. Then she straightened up. "I lost consciousness!" she added briskly.

"You just set out here on the porch a minute," the traffic cop told Rush and Mona. "She'll be all right in a jiffy." As the door closed, Randy could hear Rush saying to someone, "Yes, she's my sister. Never rode a bicycle before today." He sounded very important.

The name of the traffic cop was Mr. Wheelwright (which Randy thought was a good name for him) and his wife, Mrs. Wheelwright, was a nice fat lady with a kind heart who took Randy under her wing with the greatest pleasure.

"Well, for pity's sake," she kept clucking. "Why, you poor little mite. Why, you poor little *mite*."

The Wheelwrights' house was very interesting, though rather dim because all the windows were smothered under a profusion of potted plants. There were red geraniums, and fuchsias whose blossoms hung from their stems like costly earrings, and great overgrown begonias, and calceolarias all covered with little speckled calico pocketbooks. There were ivies, too, and rubber plants, and lots of others that Randy couldn't name, all growing furiously like plants in an African jungle. Randy secretly wondered how they ever opened the windows in this house. Maybe they just didn't bother.

Besides the plants there seemed to be a great many animals: dogs and cats, and cages and cages of birds: canaries and lovebirds, chattering and singing beside the green windows. And when they went into the bathroom upstairs, where Mrs. Wheelwright bathed Randy's cut (quite a good cut, deep and long and bloody), Randy couldn't believe her eyes. There was an alligator in the bathtub!

"My goodness" was all she could say. The alligator was about two feet long and lay half out of the water on a soapstone block, with a Mona Lisa smile on his face.

Randy was so fascinated she hardly noticed the iodine biting into her wound.

"Ouch," she said absently. "But where did you get him, Mrs. Wheelwright?"

"My sister, Ethelda, down in Florida sent him to us for a joke more'n twelve years ago. Ed, that's Mr. Wheelwright, figured the creature would die pretty soon; they usually do up here, you know. We sort of counted on it."

She put a gauze dressing on the cut and plastered it down with adhesive tape.

"Well, but he didn't die," she continued. "We fed him real good, and took care of him because after all we've got

kinda soft hearts, and first thing you know he's feeling pert
as a kitten, and he's got that great big grin on his face."

She sighed as she closed the door of the medicine chest.

"In summer Ed puts him out in a tank in the yard. But
in winter, now that he's getting s'big, we just have to keep
him in the bathtub. It makes it awful inconvenient: we
have to take our baths in the kitchen, just like there wasn't
no modern conveniences in the place."

"What's his name?" asked Randy.

"We call him Crusty," replied Mrs. Wheelwright. She
sighed again. "The Lord knows what we'll do with him
when he outgrows the bathtub. Well, time to worry about
it later. Now, honey, you come on downstairs and lay on
the davenport for a while, and I'll find you a little bite to
strengthen you. You can meet the rest of the family, too."

Were there other people in the house? Randy had heard
no voices. But the rest of the family turned out to be the
animals: a very fat old dog, her daughter and grandson;
three big grey Maltese cats, all brothers; two lovebirds,
man and wife, and five canaries whose relationships were
not explained.

The living room was full of things: tables, and lots of
chairs, all with crocheted antimacassars; pictures and pen-
nants and fans on the wall; a big melodeon at one end of
the room with very old sheet music on it; and in the wide
doorway there were portieres all made of beads which
rattled like rain on a tin roof when Mrs. Wheelwright
brushed against them. The place was so full of animals
and plants and furniture that Mr. and Mrs. Wheelwright
just walked around their house on little paths. It was rather
a stuffy, crowded way to live, Randy thought, but very

interesting and never lonesome. She lay quiet on the big, full-bodied couch that was covered with a stiff, stinging plush, like nettles. Mrs. Wheelwright brought her a frosted doughnut and a glass of root beer. The canaries sang madly, and the lovebirds screamed at each other in the customary way of lovebirds. One of the cats sat on the arm of the couch with his tail curled around his paws, and the oldest, fattest dog kept trying to sit up and beg, and falling over because of too much fat.

"That's Teeny," Mrs. Wheelwright said proudly. "She's fourteen years old."

"My sister Mona is almost fourteen, too," Randy remarked. "But not so fat for her size."

"My lands!" cried Mrs. Wheelwright in consternation. "Your brother and sister have been waiting outside all this time! They'd probably like some doughnuts, too." Deftly she made her way between tables and chairs and over cats and dogs to the front door.

Rush and Mona came in looking hungry, and sat down behaving like company.

"Are you really all right, Ran, darling?" inquired Mona as Mrs. Wheelwright bustled into the kitchen, leaving the bead portieres rattling.

"I'm fine," Randy said. "I like this place."

Mrs. Wheelwright returned with more doughnuts and root beer.

"Your little sister got a pretty bad cut," she told Rush and Mona.

"Oh, she's always doing something," Rush said between mouthfuls, and during them. Randy blushed modestly. "She broke her collarbone when she was four, and she knocked out two front baby teeth when she fell off the rocking horse the same year. And then when she was six she got stuck in a revolving door, and last year she almost got suffocated with coal gas, and—"

"And she fell out of a boat in Central Park in New York City, too," added Mona. "Nobody ever does that."

"Oh, it wasn't anything," said Randy, feeling pleased.

"Yes, and she set the house on fire once by accident," continued Rush. "And she was the only one of our family that got mumps the time we had mumps at school."

"Well!" said Mrs. Wheelwright. "Things just seem to happen to you, don't they, honey?"

Then Mr. Wheelwright came in and offered to drive Randy home in the next-door neighbor's pickup truck. But no; Randy wanted to ride her bike.

"That's right," said Rush approvingly. "After a crash they always make aviators fly again, so they won't lose their nerve."

"Only don't get too far ahead of me," begged Randy.

Before she left she thanked Mrs. Wheelwright. "Can I come and see you sometimes?" she asked.

"You come whenever you want to, honey," Mrs. Wheelwright said. "Maybe you'd like to come on Thursdays when I let the birds fly around the house. Or maybe you'd like to come on Saturdays when I bake cookies."

"Maybe I'd like to come both times," Randy suggested greedily, and Mrs. Wheelwright seemed to think that was a good idea.

Randy enjoyed the ride home. Her bicycle appeared to be repentant of its past actions and took her docilely in at the gate, down the hill, and along the drive without a single fall.

"My lands!" cried Cuffy when she saw her. "You look like the Spirit of '76!"

"The Carthage traffic cop has an alligator in his bathtub!" Randy told her.

"The *what!*" Cuffy looked startled. "You sure your head feels all right?"

But Oliver, who was getting ready for his bath, said gloomily, "A bathtub's a good place for an alligator. Not for a boy like me. Alligators *like* water."

That night Randy had her supper in bed: chicken broth, and toast, and lemon jelly. Just like a real invalid. And afterward everyone came up to see her. Mrs. Oliphant and Father made her promise to ride her bike only on the home grounds until she became more expert.

Before she turned out the light, Randy took inventory of her wounds. There were four dark bruises and a skinned knee on her right leg; five dark bruises and a scratched shin on her left. She also had a swollen wrist and a scraped elbow. But the crowning glory, the best wound, the one she valued above all others, was the deep cut on her forehead. Maybe it will leave a scar, she thought hopefully. Oh, if it only would: a distinguished little white scar that she could point to and say casually, "This? Oh, I got this the time I ran into the back of the bus."

It had been a good day, a wonderful day. She had a new bicycle, she had made new friends, and probably she was going to have a scar.

CHAPTER V

Rock-A-Bye Rush

UP ON the hill in the woods there was an oak. Of course there were a lot of oaks; dozens of them. There were birch trees, too, with bark like torn satin, and hickory trees, and elms, and pines, and big silvery beeches that looked as if they'd been poured into molds. Thousands of trees, there were. But this oak was special.

Rush had been looking for the right tree for days, now. It had to be tall, for one thing; it had to have widespread branches not too near the earth, and it had to be strong. Also it had to grow on a hill. This was it.

Once long ago Rush had built a tree house in a place where the Melendys used to spend their summers, and he had never forgotten it. It had been his own private domain and nobody had been allowed to enter it without a special invitation extended by the architect. He remembered with pleasure the privacy and power he had felt in his tree house. He remembered the way it had creaked and swayed high among the branches; and how it bucked and leaped like a ship at sea whenever the wind was strong. It had been wonderful to lie on his back in that airy, gently rocking nest and look up into the living, complicated

54

structure of leaves and branches. Why not do it all over again?

"Why not?" Father agreed. "There's a lot of wood out in the stable. Down in the furnace room, too, left over from crates. You ought to be able to find enough material."

"Be careful now, Rush," cautioned Cuffy. "I don't want no broken collarbones."

"I know just what to do for a broken collarbone," Mona said, with a glint in her eye. "They're teaching our class first aid at school." Rush had an uncomfortable suspicion that she would welcome his breaking a bone just for the pleasure of treating it.

"Rest assured that *all* my bones will be guarded as carefully as rare jewels from the Indies," said Rush. "I'm not going to have you fussing with my fractures, Mona, and putting my bones together upside down. Not a chance, pal, not a chance!"

Willy Sloper helped him with the house. There were a lot of crates, just as Father had said, and Rush and Willy made several trips up the hill carrying wood, saws, hammers, and nails. Randy and Oliver were allowed to accompany them, staggering under armfuls of planks.

All Saturday and Sunday of the third weekend that the Melendys had been living in the Four-Story Mistake, the sound of hammer beats came from the woods; and finally on Sunday evening the tree house was finished. The whole family, Cuffy, Oliver, Isaac, everybody, went up the wooded hill to inspect it.

It was an excellent tree house. They all said so, even Father. It was a square, broad platform anchored to boughs twenty feet above the earth. There was a railing round it, and wires were bound from the corner posts about the branches beneath.

"Yessir," Willy Sloper said, "can't nothin' much shake down that little roost without it's a hurricane. But I might need that ladder again sometime. You better build the foot pieces onto the trunk real soon."

Rush kept forgetting about building the foot pieces. So many things were happening. Everyday they rattled off to school in the Motor. The Carthage people made quite a lot of fun of it. They called it the Jalopy, or the Aquarium, or the Caboose-that-Got-Left-Behind. The Melendys didn't mind. They knew it was a funny-looking old thing, but they were fond of it and it got them places without quite falling apart.

They had all made friends, and school was beginning to be very interesting to them. Mona was at the head of practically everything in her class except sports and mathematics. "I think I'm going to be president pretty soon, too," she said modestly.

Rush was the best of his class in mathematics and history. "And if they had a music department, I'd be best in that," he admitted with candor.

Randy excelled only in drawing, which they didn't have often. And poor Oliver wasn't at the head of anything at all in *his* class. He confessed it freely, thought for a minute, and brightened as he added, "But me and Joseph Bryan weigh more than anybody else!"

Home was nice, too. The queer old house was comfortable and spacious; even Randy had stopped being homesick. She had built a feeding-stand for birds on the roof outside the cupola. Each day she got up early, sprinkled bread crumbs there and millet seed, and watched them come: sparrows, of course, a greedy starling, big, savage bluejays, and all the rare, shy ones: tanagers, and cardinals, and fox-brown thrushes.

Mona had pinned up all her signed photographs of actors and actresses; she was also writing a play, and learning how to knit. Rush had found the right place for his piano, and spent hours practicing whenever he wasn't up in the tree house. And Oliver, when he didn't sneak down to the cellar room, spent most of his time courting colds in the brook.

Indian summer lasted a long time that year. So long into the autumn that the violet plants beside the brook believed that spring had come again and put out new blossoms. Each day the sun shone, the birds lingered, though the trees were turning, purely out of habit, and their rose and yellow and rust looked strange and beautiful above the brilliant green grass. It was a wonderful time: almost better than spring, really, because it was rarer. Each golden day was cherished to the full, for one had the feeling that each must be the last. Tomorrow it would be winter.

The Melendys went about in shorts and bare feet, breathing the air luxuriously and hating to go indoors. Hickory trees abounded on the place, and black walnuts and butternuts. The old orchard had a russet tree whose apples tasted sweeter and sharper and better than any apples the children had ever eaten. When they were at home, they were always biting and nibbling, breaking nuts with big stones, or wandering through the high, dry grass of the orchard looking for windfalls. "I loved the old house," Randy said sadly. "But I'm afraid I'm going to love this one even better."

One day Rush came home early from school. The man from Freebush's grocery store brought him home with the delivery. Two pounds of bacon, a roast of beef, a bushel of potatoes, six cans of peaches, and Rush arrived together at eleven-thirty in the morning.

"Why, what's the matter?" inquired Cuffy, wiping her hands on her apron. "Why're you home so early? Been bad?"

"No, Cuffy," Rush said. "But Miss Holsinger thinks I've got a temperature. My throat's sore."

"Throat's sore!" exclaimed Cuffy. "Why didn't you say so this morning? You come right in and go to bed. I'll give you some aspirin and a gargle."

Rush followed her unhappily into the house. It was a lovely day and he hated to go to bed.

Except for when I swallow, I feel perfectly okay, he thought.

After a delicate invalid lunch, a long nap, and a half hour's perusal of his algebra book, Rush felt well and in need of entertainment. He went out on the landing and called for Cuffy. There was no answer. She had gone to Carthage in the Motor with Willy Sloper. Father was in New York, Rush knew; everybody else was at school. Even Isaac failed to respond to his whistle; Cuffy must have taken him to Carthage with her.

Disconsolately Rush went back to bed. Once more he studied his algebra book, unhappily. He looked at his other books in their cases, but he had read them all at least twice.

He lay back on his pillow, but it felt full of lumps, and he wasn't sleepy.

"Darn it, I'm bored!" Rush said crossly to his room. The cool, white walls stared back at him indifferently. He rolled over and gazed gloomily out his window at the black boughs of the Norway spruce. Just about now the guys in his class would be out on the field for football practice. He hated like the dickens to miss it.

The dark branches lifted a little and swayed against the window. Rush sat up.

"No one's here to tell me not to. Why don't I try it?"

He got out of bed, put on his sweater, a bathrobe and a pair of felt slippers, and opened the window. Just as he had one leg over the sill, a thought occurred to him: he went back to his bed and buried a pillow under the blankets in a lifelike mound. "Just in case," said Rush prudently. He returned to the window, straddled the sill and reached for the nearest spruce branch. It was quite easy. Feeling clever and adventurous, he reached back and closed his window. Then he continued his investigation of the tree; he had been meaning to do it for weeks. There were a great many scratchy needles and inconvenient twigs, but the boughs were not too far apart. Bleeding slightly from several scratches, with a tear in his bathrobe, and the greater portion of an abandoned bird's nest draped about his head and shoulders, Rush finally reached the bottom. First he brushed and shook himself and got rid of the pieces of bird's nest which had gone down his neck and felt exactly as if he were wearing a shirt made of shredded wheat. Then he ambled lightheartedly (and a little lightheadedly, too, owing to his temperature) across

THERE WERE A GREAT MANY SCRATCHY NEEDLES

the lawn. It was delightful to know that everybody was away. The place was his and his alone. He sang to himself as he floated across the grass, and up into the woods. He sang a good, loud sea song that he was fond of:

"But *OH* it was a cruel sight
And grieved us full sore.
Sail *HIGH* sail *LOW*
And so-o sailed we,
To see them all a-drowning
As they tried to swim to shore—
A-sailing down all on the coast of *HIGH* Barbaree!"

He scrambled up Willy Sloper's ladder, hurdled the railing of the tree house, and sat down on the floor with his back pressed against the rough substantial trunk of the oak. It was good to rest after his recent exertion. He sat very still listening to the minute, distant ringing of the fever in his ears. Beyond it there were other sounds: the sounds of a warm fall day. Leaves dropped with a whisper to the earth, and acorns plopped like heavy drops of rain. A woodpecker rapped at the trunk of the tree above Rush's head. Another pecked near by, and another, and another, and another. The woods were full of a ghostly, hollow knocking as though dozens of brittle knuckles beat upon closed doors.

He lay down flat on his back and looked up into the purpling roof of leaves. How high it was, and beyond it how tremendous was the sky. Rush felt as though he were lying on the floor of the ocean, deep, deep down. Fathomless currents stirred the leaves, and rocked his cradle. By and by he was asleep.

At half past four everybody came home in the Motor. Randy, Mona, and Oliver played prisoner's base on the lawn. Cuffy peeked into Rush's room, thought that he was sleeping, and went down to the kitchen to get supper. Willy came with her to peel the potatoes and have a good talk.

At five-thirty a procession of slate-blue clouds rose out of the west and hid the setting sun. They were thick, huge, overpowering clouds full of a mean spirit. The surprise they brought with them was a vast, boisterous wind that burst unannounced upon the world, to tear the last of Indian summer into ribbons. The children ran indoors, Willy went down cellar to get wood for the fireplaces, and Cuffy hurried out to the clothesline and gathered up armfuls of bounding, devil-possessed clothes. High in the tree house Rush curled deeper into sleep, pulling his bathrobe close about him.

"How's Rush feeling, Cuffy?" asked Mona, setting the table.

"I guess he's all right," Cuffy answered from the kitchen. "He's still asleep."

She was right about that. Rush was still asleep. Only not where she thought he was. The wind blew harder and harder. It wrenched the shutters from their catches and slapped them against the house; it blew the smoke down the chimney, and tore branches from the trees. Up in the woods something fell to the earth with a loud crash.

Rush sat up suddenly, chilled and stiff. At first he couldn't remember where he was. He was lost in a frightening turmoil of dark and wind. The very earth was rocking beneath him and overhead all he could see was strange, tossing forms and driving clouds. Absolutely terrified he put out his hand and touched the rough, solid bark of the oak. The cold sweat of relief sprang out all over him. So it wasn't the end of the world, after all. It was only his own tree house rocking in a gale!

"Boy, I better scram back to bed," Rush said to himself. "I wonder if I can climb up that spruce tree in the dark as easily as I came down it?" The thought exhausted him. Maybe he could sneak up the back stairs without being caught. He turned up the collar of his bathrobe, flung one leg over the rail, and reached out with his slippered foot for the top rung of Willy's ladder. His foot waved aimlessly at first, then searchingly, and at last frantically. There was no ladder.

"Well, gee," Rush said. He waved his foot around some more, but it met only empty space. The ladder had blown over. That must have been what woke him up.

"I could jump," he remarked without enthusiasm. He leaned over the railing and looked down. Jump? Twenty feet in the dark and into bushes? "You'd be a jackass to try it," Rush admonished himself. "You'd break something or other, and first thing you know Mona'd be practicing her first aid on you. Not much."

The next thing was to yell.

He leaned far out and shouted in the direction of the house. "Cuffy!" brayed Rush. "Oh, WILL-ee!"

But the wind and the woods were roaring like the entire Atlantic Ocean. Rush might have been a cricket chirping in a wilderness. He had yelled so hard and long that his already sore throat began to ache unbearably, and, discouraged, he sat down again on the platform, his back against the oak. There was nothing to do but wait. "Maybe I'll die up here; starve to death," he mumbled, feeling sorry for himself; but the absurdity of the statement was apparent even to him. Sooner or later somebody would come. But by that time I'll be dead of exposure, Rush thought. That wasn't so amusing. The wind howled about him, cold and violent, and only the fever in his veins kept him warm. "I probably really will get pneumonia now," he said, with a sort of triumphant gloom.

Far away, between leaves and branches, he could see the small, glittering lights of the house. They came and went, fitfully; a constellation of fireflies. Inside the house the family would be eating supper now—warm, cozy, and protected, not caring that he was alone, cold, shut out in the storm. Why didn't they come and find him? But there was a good answer to that, and Rush knew what it was. The answer was a pillow buried in a lifelike lump under the blankets of his bed. "You don't get away with much in this world," observed Rush profoundly.

Oh, it was a wild night. The oak was racked with wind: it creaked and groaned in all its limbs; cold leaves flew at Rush like bats. Overhead the torn, moon-filtered clouds raced hauntedly across the sky. What a howling, tossing, frenzied world it was! Too bad it's not Halloween, he thought. Anybody could believe in witches tonight. But Halloween had come and gone a week ago, mild as a lamb.

He shook with chill and burned with fever by turns. Against the darkness strange patterns flamed and were gone; fiery pinwheels, dancing stars, geometrical designs outlined in colored light; all the fantastic figures of a fevered imagination. Rush watched them with his teeth chattering. The Brahms Rhapsody galloped interminably through his mind in tune with the wild night. I don't think I'll ever be able to play it again, he thought, without feeling sick.

At half past eight the rain began. It was violent, like the wind, coming in great bursts and waves, cold and heavy as water pouring over a dam. He huddled against the tree, his head on his knees, his arms around his head; he had never been so wretched in his life. There was nothing left in the whole world but noise, and water, and confusion. This is how a soldier feels, Rush thought, far away in a foreign land; hiding in the dark and rain, waiting to fight. Somehow the thought made him feel braver. After all, he was lucky: there was no enemy searching for *him*, at least.

In the warm living room of the house the fire hissed and crackled; a log caved in, sending up a shower of sparks. Mona sighed over her Latin, and Randy sighed over her English grammar. Isaac whimpered in his sleep. There was no sound from Oliver; he had gone to bed long ago.

Cuffy put down her mending.

"Poor Rush," she said. "He's been sleeping all day. He ought to have some hot lemonade."

"I'll make it, Cuffy," Mona offered, glad to escape from her homework. "You go and see how he is."

Cuffy tiptoed up the stairs and opened Rush's door. She stood there in the rectangle of light cast by the hall lamp, and listened. Gracious, how still the child was! There was no sound of deep, even breathing; no restless stirring against the pillow. She frowned and went quickly over to the bed.

An instant later she came out of the room and hurried upstairs to the Office. Then to the cupola; and down again.

"Randy!" called Cuffy from the landing. "Mona! Rush isn't here! The rapscallion's gone off somewheres and left his pillow in the bed. One of you go down cellar and see if he's there! One of you go out and get Willy. Hurry!"

"I'll go," cried Randy, and rushed for the door.

"Put on your raincoat," ordered Cuffy, even in the midst of her distraction, "and take your shoes off the minute you get back. It's pouring! Now where in time did I put the flashlight?"

But Randy didn't wait. Grabbing her slicker she rushed out. The wind almost took her off her feet; the cold rain was blown against her. She ran to the stable, leaping over fallen branches and splashing through puddles. The stable door was closed and she almost broke her back getting it open. Recklessly she made her way to the narrow stairs and bumped her shin hard against the first step, but hardly even felt it, she was so frightened. A crack of light was shining under Willy's door, and his radio was going full blast: dance music loud enough to burst an eardrum!

"Willy, Willy!" shouted Randy, banging her fists against the door.

"What's the matter?" cried Willy, throwing it open. "House on fire? Someone sick? What's the matter?"

"It's Rush!" gasped Randy. "We can't find him."

Willy waited for nothing. Still wearing his old fleece-lined slippers and holding a copy of *Popular Mechanics* in one hand, he raced down the stairs beside Randy. Behind them dance music still poured lavishly out of the radio.

"He's not in the house nowheres?"

"We couldn't find him. We don't know where he is!" Randy was almost in tears. "He's got a temperature, too."

"I bet I know!" cried Willy, with a flash of inspiration. "You go on back to the house now. Go on, do like I say. Go get your feet dry. I've got my pocket flashlight with me."

A few minutes later Rush thought he heard someone calling his name. He paid no attention. Probably just fever again, he thought to himself. Or maybe it's the angel Gabriel. Bu then he heard the sound of something scraping against the tree, and saw a light shining vertically through the rain. He tottered to his feet and looked over the railing right into the ascending face of Willy Sloper.

"You look even better than the angel Gabriel to me," croaked Rush thankfully; and Willy reached out a wiry arm, helped him over the railing, half carried him down the ladder, and really did carry him all the way through the woods to the house. Willy was a swell guy. He never fussed around with whys and hows. He just carried Rush home and kept saying, "It's all right now. You're okay now. We'll have you back in your bed in a jiffy."

And in a jiffy Rush was back in bed, wearing dry pajamas, and feeling as if he had died and gone to a warm, dry heaven. The storm had put the lights out again, of course, but there was a kerosene lamp purring on the table beside him. Nobody scolded him, not even Cuffy. They seemed to take it for granted that he had been punished enough, as indeed he had.

"Are you frozen anyplace?" asked Mona eagerly. "I know exactly what to do for frostbite!"

"Sorry to disappoint you," Rush replied through the pleasant ringing in his ears, "but I'm *not* frozen anyplace. I feel swell."

Mona draped a shawl across his shoulders, Randy brought him a hot-water bottle, and Willy heaped wood on the fire. Cuffy came up with a trayful of hot things to eat: hot soup, hot ovaltine, hot milk toast.

"I feel like a very rich old lady," Rush remarked appreciatively. "My only regret is that in real life I'll never get to be a grandmother."

"Or rich either, probably," said Mona witheringly.

"Go on now," Cuffy said. "All of you. *Out!* He has to have his temperature taken before he eats these hot things. And he has to have an aspirin *afterwards*."

Rush was sick in bed for over a week with bronchitis and except for the first two days enjoyed every minute of it. Father brought him some new books, Oliver loaned him his comics, and Willy the back issues of *Popular Mechanics*. Cuffy was always making delicious streamlined things that went down his throat without bumping it. Nobody was allowed to come into the room to see him except grownups, who were tough old things, less liable to catch his germs. But Cuffy spent hours mending in the rocker beside the window; she was always good company and so was Father, who spent each evening with him, and Willy Sloper, who came for frequent conversational visits. When he was alone, Rush read and read and read. When he got tired of reading he played the gramophone or his radio. When he got tired of that he worked on his model airplanes, and when he got tired of that he added the finishing touches to a story he was writing called "The Ghost in the Dumbwaiter," and when he got tired of *that* he simply lay still and watched the swaying spruce branches against the grey sky, and listened to the music inside his head. Sometimes he just slept.

Yes, it was a fine illness. But after eight days of it he was glad to be up again; tottering weak and pale about the house. Also he retained a distinctive bass cough, more animal than human, that hung on for weeks and startled everyone who heard it. It kept him provided with free cough drops, oranges, lozenges, and whole jars of honey. He was quite sorry when he got over it.

CHAPTER VI

Clarinda, 1869

"IT'S snowing!" cried Randy one Saturday morning from her roost in the cupola. She had gone up there with a book of Father's called *Jean-Cristophe* which she didn't understand. "Real snow!" she shouted exultantly, forgetting all about the strange boy in the book and tumbling down the steps to the Office. "First I thought it was just ashes from the chimney but I watched and it melted right on the window sill!"

Rush stopped playing the piano. Mona stopped writing her play. Oliver stopped trying to draw a battle between fourteen airplanes and thirteen submarines, all on the same sheet of paper. With one accord they went downstairs, put on their coats and, as an afterthought, their galoshes, and went outdoors. None of them had ever seen snow in the country. At first it wasn't very exciting, really. The sparse, papery flakes flew down, alighted, and vanished without making any difference on the landscape.

But Oliver made a discovery.

"Look," he said, examining the snowflakes on his sleeve. "They're shaped like little sort of fuzzy stars."

Oh, everybody knew *that!*

"Didn't you really ever notice it before, Oliver?" Randy sounded astonished. Nevertheless, she ran into the house and borrowed one of the lenses from Rush's microscope and she and Oliver took turns peering through it at the snow crystals. How wonderful they were! So tiny, so perfect, down to the last point, the last feathering of frost. There were little stars, and miniature geometrical ferns and flowers, and patterns for fairy crowns, and tiny hexagons of lace. And each was different from all the others.

"How can they ever think of so many patterns?" wondered Randy, relinquishing the lens to Oliver.

"How can *who* ever think of them?" said Oliver, breathing so hard on the flake he was examining that it turned into a drop of water.

"God, I suppose," Randy answered, catching some snow on the tip of her tongue and eating it.

"Does He draw them first, or does He just go ahead and cut them out and drop them?" Oliver wanted to know.

But that was too much for Randy. Snowflakes were a mystery altogether.

"Come on," she said. "Let's go up through the woods to the top of the hill and see how it looks from up there."

By lunchtime the valley was lightly coated, like a cake with confectioner's sugar; and by half past three the snow was of a respectable depth: halfway to the tops of their galoshes. There was white fur on the antlers of the iron deer and on the melancholy boughs of the Norway spruce.

They cleared the front drive with Willy, built a snowman for Oliver and a fort for all of them. "But, gee, if we only had a sled!" Rush said finally. Oliver stopped digging, leaned thoughtfully on his spade, and in a moment or two drifted inconspicuously toward the house.

Scrape, scr-a-a-pe, went Willy's industrious shovel. The millions of little white stars twinkled down, and down, and down; an endless supply. Mona bent over and wrote her name, big, on the snow with the point of her mitten.

MONA MELENDY.

Then she stood off and looked at it. It was the kind of name that would look well in lights when she was famous. Oh, yes, of course, Mona Melendy. Isn't she wonderful? The most perfect Juliet I ever—

"Ow! Rush, you devil!" yelped Mona furiously as a wet, generous handful of snow down her back brought the glorious daydream to a close. The fight was on. Half in earnest, half in fun, they pelted each other, rolled on the ground, got soaking wet. Rush was strong, but Mona was bigger. She got him down, finally, and was sitting firmly on his chest combing her disheveled hair when she saw Oliver returning.

"Why, look what he's got!" she exclaimed, rising suddenly and liberating her victim.

"Sleds, gee whiz," murmured Rush, in awe. They were sort of funny, shabby old things with high, rusted runners, and names painted on them in fancy letters. "Snow Demon," one was called. "Little Kriss Kringle" was the other. Yes, they were strange, but never mind, they were sleds!

"Where'd you ever get them, Fatso?" inquired Rush.

"Me? Oh, I just found them," replied Oliver vaguely.

"But *where*?"

"Oh, just around."

"What do you mean *around*? I never saw any sleds lying around the Four-Story Mistake. Come on, Oliver, give us the dope, like a good guy."

"I can't," said Oliver firmly. "It's a secret."

Randy couldn't resist boasting a little. "I know where he got them," she crowed. "But I promised not to tell." And she and Oliver exchanged a wink of the greatest satisfaction and good will.

The sleds turned out to be all right, though not greased lightning by any means. Rush had an inspiration, too, and went and got two large dishpans from the house; so each of them had a suitable vehicle for traveling down a snowy hill. The dishpans were particularly exciting, because they not only descended rapidly, but spun round and round while doing so. At the bottom of the slope you rose with difficulty, staggered, and discovered that you were the exact center of a world that revolved about you like a mammoth merry-go-round. Oliver was the only one who didn't care for this. His stomach resented the spinning of the dishpan, though for some reason it did not resent being slammed down belly-whopper on a sled over and over again.

Even Willy Sloper came and joined them for a while, and the picture of him going down the slide in a dishpan, arms and legs waving like an old-fashioned windmill was one that none of them would ever forget.

"I know what let's do," Mona said, when they were all exhausted and hot and red-cheeked. "I read about it in a book. They made snow ice cream in this book. Why don't we make some?"

"How do you do it?"

"Well, first we have to beg a bottle of milk and some sugar from Cuffy. You do it, Rush. You're best at it."

"Okay," said Rush, who was hungry, trotting obediently toward the house.

"And some cups," called Mona, "and some *spoons!*"

Then she and Randy and Oliver went looking for the cleanest, purest patch of snow they could find, which was in the middle of the front lawn: untouched, unmarked, it looked as though it had been created to be eaten.

It tasted very good, too, though rather flat, later on when Rush had brought sugar and milk to mix with it. Oliver ate so much that his alert and responsive little stomach felt strange again, and he retired to the house.

Mona and Randy gathered up cups and spoons and went back to the house, too. But Rush left them and took a walk up into the woods. It was dusk, but the snow lent a strange radiance to the world. Flakes still fell, melting cold on his cheek, whispering with a feathery sound. There was no sound but their whisper, and his boots crunching softly. Isaac bounded at his heels with a white beard and ear-fringes.

"Just think," Rush said, "almost a year ago I found you. And in a snowstorm like this." He leaned down and patted Isaac, who looked up at him lovingly with one cold paw raised out of the snow.

"Let's go back," Rush said. The woods were beautiful and mysterious; but suddenly he was cold; he longed for noise, and warmth and light. Isaac understood; he turned with a little yelp of joy and galloped beside his master down the hill toward the bright windows of the kitchen.

The next day, Sunday, was a great disappointment to them all. During the night, by some strange alchemy, the snow had turned to rain. The spruce trees looked dreary and uncomfortable, like monstrous, wet crows. Only Oliver took any pleasure in the morning, slopping about and digging in the dissolving snow. The rest of them did their chores, their homework, and snapped at each other. After dinner when they started a noisy game of dumb-crambo in the living room Father came out of the study and asked them to go up to the Office. "I can't even hear my typewriter," he complained, "let alone my own thoughts!"

Silent and out of sorts they retired to the Office. By now it was pouring. What is worse than a rainy Sunday afternoon when you've eaten a heavy dinner?

Randy sat down at the piano. She played the piece that Rush had taught her. It was a simple air by Bach, and the oftener she played it the better she liked it. First she played it as if she were very happy, and then as if she were very sad. (It sounded wonderful when played sadly, so she did it several times.) She also made it into a dance; into a thunderstorm, a picnic on the first day of spring, a funeral march, and a witch's lament. It sounded beautiful to her in all its transformations, she never got tired of it, but after half an hour Mona looked up from her book and said, "If you play that tune one more time, Ran, I'm going to start screaming and I don't think I'll be able to stop!"

"Oh, all right, if you feel like that." Randy folded her hands in her lap and sat very stiff on the piano bench. She hoped she looked deeply hurt, and stared coldly at the cutout pictures on the wall above the piano.

"Well, that's funny," she exclaimed a moment later, standing up and peering closer at the wall.

"H-mmm?" Mona's voice came vaguely from the distant regions of Castle Blair.

"I said, well, that's very funny," repeated Randy remembering to sound offended.

"What is?" Rush looked up languidly.

"Why, goodness! Come here, Rush! Look!"

"I don't see anything," said Rush, standing beside her. "Just those same old pictures pasted up. I practically know them by heart."

"No, no," Randy was excited. "See how the paper's sort of broken along here?"

"It's just a crack between the boards," Rush said.

"No, I don't think so," Randy persisted. "Look how it goes: up to here, and then across to there, and then down again. And look, there's kind of a bulge on that side. Like a hinge!"

"Like a hinge," repeated Rush, light dawning. "Creepers, Ran! Do you suppose it could be a door?"

"That's what I think," agreed Randy, as solemn as an archaeologist who has discovered the relics of a lost primitive race.

"Come on, kids, help move the piano out so we can see." But they didn't need to be asked; already they were pushing and tugging and the piano moved slowly outward, squealing on its casters.

"Where's your knife, Rush? Why don't you slit the paper along those cracks?" suggested Mona.

"No, let Randy," said Rush honorably, unsheathing the

wicked-looking blade of his scout knife. "After all, she discovered it."

Rush was wonderful, Randy thought. Almost trembling with excitement she slit the ancient paper along the crack upward from the floor. But she wasn't tall enough to reach along the top.

"It's a door all right," whispered Rush, as though an enemy lurked beyond the partition. "But it's nailed shut: I can feel the nailheads under the paper. Here, hand over the knife, Randy. I'm taller. I'll do the top."

"Think how long it's been shut," Mona said, awed. "The pictures on this part of the wall are the oldest in the Office; I've noticed that before. There's a date down here above this newspaper engraving that says 1875!"

"What do you think's behind the door, Mona?" said Oliver, looking a little worried.

"Ah, that's a question, Fatso," Rush told him. "Maybe gold, maybe jewels, maybe a rattrap, maybe nothing."

"Not—not anything alive?" Oliver looked relieved.

"After almost seventy years? Not likely."

"Maybe a ghost," said Randy ghoulishly. "Maybe a skeleton hanging from the rafters."

"Mona?" Oliver's fat hand crept into hers.

"They're just joking, darling. Of course, there's nothing like that." But she didn't sound too sure herself.

"Funny there doesn't seem to be a trace of a latch or a handle of any kind," said Rush, feeling along the right side of the door with his long, sensitive fingers. "But I *think*— hmmm—I think *maybe* if I dig a hole just here with the point of my knife I might—just possibly—yes! It is! Look there's a keyhole!"

A keyhole!

"You look first, Randy," Rush said nobly.

"I'm almost scared to," Randy confessed. But then she knelt down and glued her eye to the keyhole while the others held their breaths.

"For heaven's sake!" she exclaimed.

"What do you see?" They all asked it at the same time.

"Are we ever dumb!" said Randy.

"Why, what do you see?" Oliver was dancing up and down with impatience.

"I see a window," Randy replied slowly. "I can see the spruce branches beyond it."

"What else?"

"Just floor and some wall: it's got blue-flowered wallpaper on it. But are we ever dumb!"

"I don't see why," said Rush, gently but firmly pushing her out of the way so that he could get a good look himself.

"Well, because we know there are dormer windows all around the roof," Randy explained. "Twelve of them there are: three on each side. You can walk around the house outdoors and count them if you want to. Now just look at the Office. How many windows do you see?"

"Seven," said Mona. "I catch on. Three windows on the west wall; two apiece on the north and south. None at all on the east; just plain wall and pasted-up pictures." She knocked on the wall. "And listen how hollow it sounds. Why didn't we ever notice!"

"Unobservant," Rush told her. "And dumb, just like Randy says. Very, very dumb."

"But not even Father noticed," Mona said. "Not even Cuffy."

"And you can't call *them* dumb!" Oliver was shocked at the mere idea.

"No, you certainly can't," Rush agreed. Suddenly he stood up. "Listen, kids. I'm going to get a hammer and a pair of pliers: we've got to get this door open. Oliver, you go find the library paste. Mona and Randy, you'll have to patch the places I tear in the paper. This must be kept secret, do you understand?"

They all understood perfectly. There had never been any doubt in their minds about that.

"Because who knows what we'll find when we open it," Rush continued darkly. "We *might* find a skeleton at that, or—or a torture chamber, or—"

"Or a ghost," repeated Randy, as a chill ran over her scalp.

Oliver looked dubious.

"Ghosts!" scoffed Mona. "Honestly, Randy! And at your age." Nevertheless, her cheeks were pink, her eyes shining with excitement.

"I move we take a vow of secrecy. A blood vow," Rush said. "What do you think?"

"Oh, yes, a blood vow!" cried Randy, with a rapturous leap. "The only other blood vow we ever took was when we swore not to tell Cuffy or Father that we'd been exposed to whooping cough that time."

"Well, they just would have worried, and anyway we never got it," said Rush, as if that had justified the act. "Now, who has a pin?"

Mona had a safety pin in the ripped hem of her skirt.

Providentially she hadn't mended it days ago when she was supposed to.

"But first it has to be sterilized," she insisted from the depth of her first-aid wisdom. So they sterilized the pin in a match flame. Of course Mona knew that the whole performance was nonsense but there *was* something rather solemn about the way they pricked their thumbs and made a scarlet X on a piece of paper opposite their names.

Mona and Randy, and Rush, that is. Oliver was firm in declining to yield his blood to the enterprise, so finally they had to let him use red water color instead.

"Though it's not really legal and binding," Rush warned him.

"I don't see why it matters," Oliver maintained stoutly. "Just two different kinds of juice, that's all. You can't tell the difference on the paper."

"But it's the principle of the thing," Rush argued weakly. "Oh, well, nuts. I'm going down to get the pliers and hammer now, and we'll get to work."

What an afternoon they had! It took ages to get the nails out; they were old and rusty, and had been in the wood so long they had almost become a part of it. Each one squeaked protestingly as Rush yanked it out.

In the middle of all this they heard Cuffy coming up the stairs and had to shove the piano back into place at once. There was a scuffle as Rush and Mona returned to their books, Oliver to his drawing, and Randy sat down on the floor and covered the nails and hammer with her skirt. Four scarlet faces confronted Cuffy as she heaved into view. "What mischief are you up to?" she inquired suspiciously, looking at them.

"Us? Nothing," replied Randy. And a loud, nervous giggle escaped from her.

"We-e-e-l-l—" Cuffy was skeptical. Still the place looked no more upset than usual, and nobody seemed to be crying, so maybe it was all right. "I just came up to see if any of you would like to lick the bowl. I've just made a chocolate cake for supper and there's lots of frosting left over."

What was the matter with them? They followed her so politely down the stairs, almost as if they were reluctant to come, instead of racing and bumping into one another, each in an attempt to get there first, as they had always done on similar occasions. And when they did get there they lapped up the chocolate fast as if they wanted to get it over with. Even Oliver failed to follow his customary procedure of licking his spoon so slowly that he could hold it up when everyone else had finished and say, "Look at all I've got left!" Yes, something was up, no doubt, but Cuffy was too busy to bother about it now. The children thanked her politely, if hastily, and lunged for the stairs, racing and bumping, each in an attempt to get there first. Cuffy sighed. That was more natural.

By four o'clock it was almost dark, but Rush wouldn't let anyone turn on the lights. Instead he went down to his room and got his flashlight and worked by the light of that. "This is much safer," he told them. "Less revealing." Randy secretly thought he just liked it better that way: it made the whole enterprise more dramatic. She didn't blame him; she liked it better that way herself.

"The Egyptians used to blow anthrax dust into the cracks of the royal tombs when they sealed them," Rush recounted with relish. "Whoever broke them open was supposed to get the disease and die in agony a few days later."

"What's anthrax?" said Randy. "It sounds like something Cuffy might use in the kitchen."

"I trust not," replied Rush, with the dignity demanded by the setting. "It's a very bad disease. Cows get it, I think. Well, anyway, *inside* the tombs they put a spell on all the gold and jewels and stuff, so that any robber or explorer, or anybody who fooled around with them would meet a dire and dreadful fate. Even if it was thousands of years later."

They were silent, thinking of the old tombs: each with its sarcophagus staring into the dark.

The sleety rain brushed the windows, the spruce branches sighed funereally in the wind, and the last nail came out of the door.

"There!" said Rush. He stood up, put the tip of the pliers into the keyhole and pulled gently. At first the door refused to budge, but after a moment or two it yielded gingerly. Rush only opened it a crack; then he handed the flashlight to Randy.

"Madam," he said, "the honor is yours. You go in alone first."

What? After all that talk about skeletons, and ghosts, and anthrax dust, and ancient Egyptian curses? Oh, no, Randy wasn't going through that doorway by herself.

"You come in with me, Rush," she insisted. "Right beside me. And Mona and Oliver you stay close behind."

"Okay, ready?" Rush opened the door and slowly, half fearfully they stepped into the secret chamber. The windows admitted only the frail, pearly glow of a wet twilight, and Rush flashed his light into the room. It was a long, narrow room, they saw: merely the sliced-off end of an attic, but it had five windows of its own and the walls and even the ceiling were covered with the pretty old-fashioned blue-flowered paper. Rush flashed the lamp more thoroughly about the room.

Who was that!

Randy screamed. Even Rush made a startled sound, and Mona and Oliver leaped back into the Office as though they had been shot. Randy was right on their heels.

"A ghost, I saw a ghost!" she was gasping. "I knew there'd be a ghost, and there was!"

Oliver began to cry.

"No, no, kids. Come back!" called Rush. "It's only a picture! That's all it is. Honest. Just a big picture. Come on back and see."

Reluctantly they went back into the room. As for Oliver, he just peeked around the edge of the door until he was sure.

It was a picture, all right. Life-size, too, and set in the heaviest, fanciest, dustiest gold frame any of them had ever seen. It was a portrait of a young girl, almost a child; she might have been anywhere from twelve to sixteen, though her clothes were grown-up, old-fashioned clothes. She wore a dark-red dress with a tiny waist and a long full skirt, and lots of buttons, and loops, and fringes all over it. The artist hadn't missed a single one. Her head was bent slightly to one side, cheek resting on one finger in a sentimental attitude. Her great mane of dark ringlets fell sideways, too, like heavy tassels on a curtain, and in her half-opened, curly little mouth each tooth was painted carefully, white and gleaming as a pearl. In her right hand she held a rose about the size of a head of Boston lettuce, with a big tear of dew clinging to its petals. Below her left hand (the one that supported her cheek), her elbow was poised upon a marble balustrade. She was painted against a classic background, with what appeared to be a mighty thunderstorm sweeping across the sky.

"Who is she?" whispered Randy, in awe.

"Why's she standing in the middle of a cemetery?" said Oliver.

"That's not a cemetery, Fatso," Rush explained. "That's just a lot of ruined Greek columns in the background."

"Why're they ruined? Did a bomb drop?"

"No, they're just old; they fell to pieces."

"Oh. Well, why's she standing in the middle of all those busted columns?"

"Search me. In those days people were always painting people besides temples and ruins and stuff."

"Look," said Mona. She leaned down. Attached to the frame at the bottom of the picture was a small gold plate with something engraved on it. Mona dusted it off with the tip of her finger.

" 'Clarinda,' " she read aloud. "That's her name, I suppose. Just 'Clarinda,' and then a number, or a date I guess it is: 1869."

"Clarinda, 1869," said Rush thoughtfully. "Who was she, do you think? I bet she was a Cassidy! Clarinda Cassidy; very euphonious. It goes with all those curls. She looks kind of nice, though, doesn't she? I wonder how she could ever bend over without snapping right in half. Her waist looks about as big around as a doughnut."

"Why do you suppose she was ever nailed up in this room all by herself," said Randy, "all these years and years?"

That was a mystery no one could explain. They stood there in a little silent cluster staring at that tilted head, that narrow waist, that pearly smile. It had been a pretty exciting day altogether. First a hidden door; and then a secret room which had been closed for seventy years, and now an imprisoned maiden in a golden frame. Clarinda, 1869. What more could you ask on a wet Sunday?

A piercing blast from the kitchen shattered the stillness. Cuffy's police whistle. That meant it was time for Oliver's supper; time for Randy to set the table, and for Mona to clean the Office, since it was her week. Hurriedly, they left the secret room, closed the door, and shoved the piano back in place. Like conspirators, they separated in the directions of their various tasks. Rush's pockets were full of rusty nails that had to be disposed of; Mona remained in the Office with the lights on, hurriedly pasting back torn strips of paper so old that they kept crumbling like ashes in her fingers.

"My," said Cuffy at suppertime. "What in the world was you doing all afternoon? I thought I heard furniture being pushed around, and then everything quiet for hours, and then a lot of squeals and a kind of stampede. Some new kind of game?"

"Sort of, Cuffy," Randy said uncomfortably, with her fingers crossed under the table. It was true in a way, wasn't it?

Rush seemed to have developed a sudden consuming interest in the Cassidy family.

"Fourteen children you said, didn't you, father? I wonder what happened to them all!"

"Somebody or other told me about one of them who's still alive. A rich old gentleman out west someplace: hasn't been back in forty years," said Father. "There may be others scattered about, and doubtless many descendants."

"Why didn't they hang onto this swell place, I wonder?" Rush said. "I should think they'd have wanted to keep it in the family."

Father shrugged his shoulders; that was a question. "Perhaps they thought it was a funny old place; aesthetically it's sort of a freak, you know. I bought it through the agents of the estate of the two daughters who owned the property: two old spinsters they were; lived here till they died a few years back."

"What were their names, father?" Rush put down his fork. So did Mona. So did Randy.

"The old ladies'? Well, let's see. One was named Minnie, or Lizzie. Lizzie, I believe, and the other—"

"Not Clarinda, by any chance?" Rush demanded.

"Clarinda? No, it was Christabelle. I remember because the contrast of the two names seemed so marked. Why on earth should it have been Clarinda?" Father wanted to know.

"Oh, I—I just read the name someplace," Rush said lamely. "It's an old-fashioned name and I just thought—" But he didn't have to cross his fingers under the table, for it was the simple truth.

That night the children dreamed all night about Clarinda and the secret room. Mona and Randy and Rush, that is. Oliver dreamed that he was driving a Greyhound bus full of policemen across the Brooklyn Bridge.

CHAPTER VII

The Show

IT WAS queer the way the children kept disappearing nowadays. Cuffy couldn't understand it. Right in the house, too; she never saw them go out. She would hear them, noisy as usual, playing in the Office and then all of a sudden absolute stillness. When she went up to see what was going on there would be nobody. Nobody at all. Funny, did she only imagine that she heard a smothered whisper, the ghost of a giggle somewhere near by? But where? The cupboards were empty (or rather, they were full of everything under the sun except children); there was nobody under the tables, or behind the piano, which Rush had moved out from the wall a little, because he said it gave a better light, or even up in the cupola.

Sometimes there would be one child left in the Office. Oliver usually. But when she asked him where the others were he simply looked surprised and answered truthfully: "The others? Why, they were here a little while ago."

Cuffy just gave up.

The truth, as you have guessed, is that they spent a lot of time closeted in Clarinda's room. In the first place, they had to clean it, and that had taken two rainy afternoons after school and the better part of the next Saturday. Randy and Mona scrubbed the floor, and Rush, at the risk of breaking his neck, washed all the windows, sitting outside on the sills and leaning back against nothing like a professional window cleaner. Whenever he saw anybody, Willy, Cuffy, Father, or anybody innocently chopping wood or hanging out clothes, or something, he would drop into the room, crouch on the floor, and hiss, "Sh-h. They mustn't see! They mustn't guess!"

Oliver was given a dustcloth and told to dust. This he did in his own fashion, which meant that Mona followed him with another dustcloth and did it all over again. Everybody helped with the walls and ceiling, brushing away the immemorial cobwebs and soft dust with brooms and mops wrapped in cheesecloth. But when it came to waxing the floor Cuffy got suspicious and they had to wax the whole Office floor as well, just to put her off the track. Oh, how their backs ached that night. Oliver fell asleep over his supper, and to Mona's drowsy mind the sentences in her French grammar were as indecipherable as Aramaic symbols. But the reward was worth the labor. The room was beautiful in the daylight, with its faded, still-gay wallpaper, its five sparkling windows and shining floor; and Clarinda, properly dusted, glowing in her golden frame and ruby dress. The room appeared even lovelier than it was because they themselves had discovered and restored it.

"But it needs furniture," Mona said. The morning sunlight flooded the room; it was a dazzle of light, a wonderful, cozy place to sit in. But what to sit on? They couldn't remove any of the Office furniture without Cuffy discovering it, and half or at least a quarter of the room's charm was its secrecy. The best they could do was to smuggle in two orange crates and a footstool to be used as chairs; but these did nothing to offset the elegance of Clarinda or the shining room. "One of these days," Randy decided, "we'll have to tell Father and Cuffy and see what can be done."

In the meantime they used it as a meeting place: a sort of clubhouse. "Sh-sh," Rush would warn, as though it were a matter of the gravest danger. "Oliver, stand guard at the head of the stairs, will you? Come on, Mona, help me with the piano." Then the door would be opened quietly and they would tiptoe into the room. Their wonderful, secret room.

One day Mona called a meeting there. A special meeting, for she had an important suggestion to make. Usually the business at hand was nothing that couldn't have been discussed anywhere; and in any case it was always rapidly abandoned and forgotten in favor of games or irrelevant conversation. But this was an exception.

"Sit down, all of you," commanded Mona regally, taking the footstool for herself. "Oliver, you'd better sit on the floor beside Isaac. Everybody comfortable? Okay. Now. I've called this meeting because I have a plan to propose. I think a very timely and important plan. A—a sort of campaign, in fact."

"Listen to the president of the D.A.R.," said Rush. He couldn't help teasing her; her imitation of a chairwoman was so unconscious and so perfect. All she needed, he thought, was a bunch of orchids, and some eyeglasses, and a big hat.

"Now, Rush," objected Mona, but her composure wasn't in the least disturbed. "Look, this is the thing. We all know there's a war, don't we?"

Yes, they all knew that!

"And we want to do something about it, don't we? To help, I mean."

Naturally. But what could they do?

"I have it all planned," said Mona excitedly, forgetting to be a club president as she sprang to her feet and upset the footstool. "This is my campaign. First of all, paper. We must collect tons of paper. The government needs it."

"What for?" inquired Oliver.

"Oh, I don't know. They just need it, that's all. Randy, you can be in charge of the paper campaign. And then metal. Tin cans and tooth-paste tubes and—and, well, metal. Rush can be in charge of that. Oliver can collect tinfoil. And besides that—"Mona looked at them sternly— "if you want to be really patriotic you must all let me practice my first aid on you."

"Ah, a real sacrifice," moaned Rush.

"I'll be in charge of the knitting too," continued Mona imperturbably. "All of you must learn."

"Me?" cried Rush. "Knit?"

"Why not?" said Mona. "This is war. And bonds. We must all buy lots of Defense Bonds."

"Bonds!" said Rush. "Where do you get that? My allowance has to be stretched to the breaking point in order to buy even a Defense Stamp once a week."

Mona's eyes began to shine. She was getting to the best part of the plan.

"I've thought it all out. And I've decided we should have a show!"

"Charge admission, you mean?" Randy looked a little shocked. "We never did before."

"Of course charge admission, silly. That's the whole point. So we can buy a Defense Bond."

Randy saw that that made a difference. "You can do a dance or two," Mona told her, "and Rush can play the piano, and Oliver—"

"I can turn somersaults," Oliver suggested hopefully. "I can almost do a cartwheel, sometimes."

"No, you can be in the play I'm writing," said Mona, genius burning.

"Only I don't want to be the queen's baby like last time," said Oliver uncompromisingly.

"You won't have to be. You can be a soldier or a robber or something. Yes, I think a robber."

"Boy!" agreed Oliver wholeheartedly.

Everybody was pleased with the idea. It had been too long since they had had a show.

"And Randy can design the costumes; Cuffy and I'll help make them. She can design the sets, too, and Rush and Willy can make those. Rush, you can plan the musical background. We'll get Willy to change the records when we need them."

"The trouble is we're always limited to only four characters when we have plays," Rush said.

"What's the matter with four? You can use the same person twice, if you know how."

"You used me three times in the last play," Randy remembered. "I was the nurse, and the beggarwoman, and the detective."

"What's this opus going to be called?" Rush wanted to know.

"It's a fantasy," Mona told him. "It combines all the best features of Hans Andersen, Grimm's *Fairy Tales, The Arabian Nights,* and Superman. It's called *The Princess and the Parsnip.*"

"And who, if I may ask, is to have the part of the princess?" inquired Rush wickedly.

"Well-uh. Why, I thought I—I mean—" Mona floundered.

"Skip it. I was only kidding. Of course you'll be the princess. Who else? You're the only one in the bunch who can act. You're good, and we all know it," said Rush graciously.

"When will we have it?" asked Randy, with an excited bounce.

"How about the week before Christmas? Maybe the Saturday before. It'll be holidays then and we'll have plenty of time."

All that now remained was to ask the co-operation of Father and Cuffy and Willy. And that was gladly granted, as they had known it would be.

Before long the house was humming with exciting activity. They'd almost forgotten what fascinating work it was to build a show. Mona wandered about the grounds like Duse, reciting her lines out loud. Rush practiced furiously. Randy composed two dances: one to the Golliwog's Cakewalk, and one to The Girl with the Flaxen Hair. Also she made water-color sketches of costume designs. There was always a long streak of purple or green at the corner of her mouth because she couldn't remember not to chew her paintbrush when she was thinking.

They had rehearsals every few minutes. Oliver learned his lines first thing and recited them with all the expression of a granite slab. "No, no," Mona would tell him, exasperated. "The way you say 'Your Highness, the Baron Hackensack demands your immediate execution' sounds just as if you were saying 'No, thank you, I don't care for any more corned-beef hash.' " Poor Oliver, he tried; but it was obvious that his talents did not lie in the direction of the drama. Rush was wonderful in his part, or rather, both his parts. Almost as good as Mona herself. And Randy was what theatrical critics describe as "adequate."

Yards of colored cheesecloth billowed over the Office table, and very wet posters executed by Randy lay drying all over the floor. You had to move about with extreme caution. Down in Cuffy's room there was a great overflowing box of odds and ends that Mrs. Oliphant had sent to them some time ago. It was a treasure trove! In it there were crumpled bits of gold and silver lamé, hardly tarnished at all; chiffons in purple and green and blue, scraps of lace, beaded georgette, a huge red satin petticoat, a velvet basque the color of a pansy, and two large pieces of silk encrusted with sequins! One was gold, and one was midnight blue: dazzling, extravagant things that cried out to be used, worn, admired. In fact it was really because of the sequins that Mona had first decided to write a play. With such exotic material at hand it seemed a sin to waste it.

The invitations were sent out at once. One to Mrs. Oliphant, of course. One to the Janeway family in New York, and two other families there, and to all their Carthage school friends, and the principal, Mr. Coughing, and his wife, and the Wheelwrights, and Mr. and Mrs. Purvis, and several other people. It was too much to hope that they'd all come.

Next they went to work on the program. Rush typed them on Father's machine.

THE MELENDYS' CHRISTMAS SHOW

I.   Piano solo by Rush Melendy
     Chorale ....Johann S. Bach
II. Dance by Miranda Melendy
     Golliwog's Cakewalk ....Claude Debussy
III. Piano solo by Rush Melendy
     Intermezzo ....Johannes Brahms
IV. Dance by Miranda Melendy
     The Girl with the Flaxen Hair ..Claude Debussy
V.   The Princess and the Parsnip
     A play in three acts by Mona Melendy

CAST OF CHARACTERS

Princess Glamorosa .... Mona Melendy
Lady Esmeralda .... Miranda Melendy
The Witch Sourpuss .... Miranda Melendy
Prince Paragon .... Rush Melendy
Baron Hackensack .... Rush Melendy
Baron Hackensack's accomplice ..... Oliver Melendy
Soldier .... Oliver Melendy
Messenger .... Oliver Melendy
Bloodhound .... Oliver Melendy
Second Bloodhound .... Isaac Melendy
      Scene 1: A forest near Glamorosa's castle.
      Scene 2: Interior of the castle.
      Scene 3: The castle roof—midnight.

Randy painted little pictures of Glamorosa on the covers of the programs and stitched the pages together with gold thread. They looked very pretty and professional.

There was some debate as to how much admission price they should charge. Mona thought it ought to be a dollar. "For our country, and all," she said.

"A *dollar!*" cried Randy, scandalized. "Nobody would be able to come!"

"A dollar for grownups and fifty cents for children, I mean."

But even that seemed far too high. In the end they decided to charge fifty cents for grownups and twenty-five for children.

"And we can get somebody from school, Pearl Cotton or someone, to take charge of the ticket selling," said Mona.

The great day approached. The sliding doors between the dining and living rooms had been opened wide, and the stage set constructed in the dining room. The Melendys had to eat the last few meals before the play in the kitchen. Standing up, too, or perched on tables, because all the chairs in the house were now arranged in rows in the living room. Would there be enough of them? That was the question. The armchairs were grouped together at the back like a family of bears. The dining-room chairs stood in a righteous and unyielding row in the middle, and beside them the three Melendy rockers tipped jovially at different angles, like rowdy people laughing, splitting their sides, at some secret joke. In front of these there was a strange assortment: kitchen chairs, and odd upstairs ones, and the big couch and the little yellow brocade love seat;

old and young, spare and fat, in a sort of Memorial Day parade. At the very front were Oliver's two small chairs, all the footstools in the house, and some packing boxes somberly draped in steamer rugs. These were for the littlest children in the audience.

Side by side waited the chairs, transfixed, struck dumb before the beauty of the stage set confronting them. Rush and Willy had built the backdrop out of beaverboard, and Randy had painted it. A lonely forest scene: dozens of pale-blue tree trunks and showers of blue leaves. At the right an opening among them disclosed the misty pinnacles of a castle. On the floor the old green rug from Father's study was arranged in mossy folds; and soft blue cheesecloth curtains hung at either side of the wide door. The girls had dyed the cheesecloth themselves, and their blue hands had horrified people for days afterward.

Randy kept wandering into the living room; sinking first into one chair and then into another, regarding with awe the beauty of her handiwork. And this was only the first set, too. Think of that. Behind the forest scene there was the interior of the palace, with a tapestry painted on its wall and a window containing a piece of cloud and a sun with as many petals as a daisy. A throne went with that one, made out of Father's old Morris chair and a bedspread. And then there was the night scene! It was the best of all. Against its dark background were gold and silver constellations, fire-tailed comets, Saturn poised within his rings, and a moon as big as a bicycle wheel. And the magic thing, the really super thing about it was that it was painted with phosphorescent paint! At a given signal Willy was to turn off the lights and the audience would find

themselves gazing at a moon and stars that glowed in the
darkness with a green, unearthly light. Oh, it was almost
too much! They had never, never staged a production so
beautifully before. Maybe we should have charged a dollar
after all, thought Randy.

Yes, and the costumes! Mrs. Oliphant's sequins and gold
lamé added an *Arabian Nights'* opulence to them. Mona
was going to look wonderful in her splendid robes: a real
princess. You couldn't believe it, looking at her now. She
was wearing her oldest sweater and skirt, and her hair was
wound up on dozens of little metal curlers. "I'm going to
leave them on all day and sleep in them all night, and only
take them off just before the performance tomorrow,"
she said.

"You'll have a mighty sore scalp," Cuffy warned her.

"It'll be worth it," Mona said in an exalted voice. "Anything's worth it if my hair just curls enough."

"All for Art," remarked Rush. He was trying on the
mustache he had made out of a dime-store hair switch
which he had to wear as Baron Hackensack. He played two
roles: that of the villain, and that of the hero. It made it
difficult, since both could never be on the stage at the
same time. The prince was forced to cry "Hark! I hear
Hackensack and his odious henchman [Oliver] approach-
ing. He shall not find me here!" Or Hackensack muttered,
"Yonder goes Paragon the prince. Take cover, men. This
is not the moment for our reckoning." And in the end the
battle to the death between Hackensack and the prince
had of necessity to take place behind the scenes, with
Willy clashing the carving knife against a pot lid, and
Rush uttering the dying groans of Hackensack as he ripped

off the black mustache and crimson mantle (Mrs. Oliphant's petticoat) of the villain, and replaced the velvet doublet (Mrs. Oliphant's basque), and jeweled crown of the hero. It was during this final scene that Willy turned out the lights and the phosphorescent moon was revealed. Everything had to be done very fast and with perfect coordination, like juggling, and by the time of the dress rehearsal they were all pretty good at it.

The next morning was strange as a dream. Randy couldn't eat her breakfast. Her stomach felt queer and unfriendly. Mona, her head still bristling, as Rush said, like artillery in ambush, wandered about the house, her lips moving as she whispered her lines. She looked pale and frightened, but everyone knew that when the time came she would suddenly blossom, come to life like a rose and make the part of the princess into something fascinating and important. Rush pretended to be perfectly calm; perhaps he really was, you couldn't tell with him. And Oliver? Well, Oliver just quietly went away from it all and retired to his cellar room with a box of toy battle equipment and some apples. He knew what was best for him.

Everyone else took part in the preparation. Even Father. With Rush he went out into the woods and cut big branches of evergreen to decorate the living room, and then with Willy to help them they somehow got the piano down from the Office to the living room beside the sliding doors.

Cuffy had baked hundreds of cookies; there were trays of them cooling all over the kitchen, and if anybody so much as looked hungrily at one of them she banished him sternly from the premises. And there was punch. The old china salad bowl was full of it, and so were the two cut-glass pitchers, the biggest mixing bowl, and several saucepans. Delicious punch, the color of garnets, with little islands of pineapple and orange floating on top.

Shortly after three the people began to come. Randy in her flannel bathrobe saw the first car from the window of Mona's bedroom where she was to dress. Her stomach gave a sort of leap and turned over. She swallowed dryly and said, "Here come the first ones."

"Who?" asked Mona, beginning to take the curlers off at last.

"Wait a minute. Let's see. Father's out on the front steps to meet them. Why, it's Mrs. Oliphant! And she has one two three four five people with her!"

"Three dollars' worth," observed Rush in a mercenary tone from the next room where he and Oliver were dressing.

Next came a taxi which disgorged the whole Janeway family from New York. Six of them. Randy was just stopped in time from throwing open the window and yelling to them.

"Not now," said Mona severely. "It would spoil the mood!"

"Oh, all right. And there come the Purvises in the garbage truck; and right behind is Mr. Coughing's black sedan, and—"

"Randy!" There was such consternation in Mona's voice that her sister whirled from the window.

"What's the matter?"

"My hair! *Look* at it. What'll I do?"

It did look queer. It stood out in a great wiry muff all over Mona's head.

"I can't go on," she kept wailing just like a real actress. "I cannot go on, looking like this!"

Rush came and stood in the doorway. "Whe-e-ew!" he whistled with astonishment. "The Brillo queen!"

"Oh, go away," said Mona tearfully. "What shall I do, Ran? The more I brush the more it stands up."

"Wait a minute. I'll get Cuffy," said Randy soothingly. "If anybody can fix it, Cuffy can."

She ran down the back stairs in her soft ballet slippers. The house was humming like a wasps' nest. The front door kept opening and shutting, opening and shutting, and there were festive bursts of talk and laughter as still more people arrived. Cuffy, mercifully, was in the kitchen prowling about arranging things. She was wearing her best black satin dress, and a dusting of pure-white powder on her rosy face.

"Lands, I hope I made enough cookies to feed that mob," murmured Cuffy, looking up abstractedly. "There must be more'n fifty of 'em already. And by the way, why aren't you ready? It's twenty to four and you know you're scheduled to start at four."

"Something awful's happened," Randy told her. "Mona's hair. It—it won't lie down!"

"Great day in the morning!" cried Cuffy, rushing for the stairs. "I told her she shouldn't leave them blame things on so long. Bring a bowl of water up with you, Randy, and then hustle right into your costume. Oh, and first bring me the wire hairbrush from my bureau."

These things being done, Randy hustled. Feverishly she

put on the costume she and Cuffy had made for the Golli-wog dance. It was a one-piece union suit dyed blue, and the headdress was made out of a blue dry mop attached to a stocking skullcap. She also had blue mittens, blue socks, and her old blue ballet slippers. Mona directed her make-up.

"Put calamine lotion all over your face, Ran. Then talcum powder. It should be white as chalk." Mona's voice came jerkily and her head bobbed under the vigorous strokes of Cuffy's brush. "Now put blue around the eyes. It's there in that little box; and then a big red mouth that turns up at the corners. Here, let me do it. I've had more practice." Cuffy stood waiting, brush in hand. Already the wild hair had begun to subside a little. Maybe it would be all right.

As the finishing touches were being applied, there was a knock at the door. "Listen, folks," said Willy's husky voice. "It's five past a'ready. The folks is all here. Every chair's taken. How soon ya goina start?"

"Right now," called Rush from his room. He appeared briefly in the doorway. "Keep your fingers crossed," he said, "and make it snappy, Ran. You be in the wings wait-ing so you can go on just as soon as they get through applauding my first piano solo."

"If they applaud," said Mona, still smarting from that remark about "the Brillo queen."

Listening, they could hear the noisy murmur of the voices downstairs; the sudden clatter of handclapping, and then stillness. And now very round and clear came the first notes of the Bach Chorale. Randy stole down the back stairs; a thin, blue elf with a pounding heart.

In the dim dining room Oliver, wearing his first costume, was lying on the floor playing with a toy tank. Willy Sloper, in his best suit, was leaning against the dining-room table with his hands clasped in front of him and his head bowed. Every time he shifted his weight, or moved about, one of his shoes gave a loud, healthy chirp like a cricket.

"Why, Randy, I thought you was a little blue dandelion," whispered Willy poetically. "Plays good, don't he?" he added, jerking his head in the direction of the music.

"Wonderful!" agreed Randy fervently. The lovely air came out as sure and calm and strong as though Rush had been playing it all by himself in the Office. Randy envied him. Looking down she believed that she could see the second button of the union suit bumping up and down above her panic-stricken ribs.

The music ceased, and there was tremendous applause. It went on and on like the sea, roaring interminably. Randy's head felt miles away from her feet. It felt light as a balloon, and her feet felt rooted to the earth; and between her head and feet there was nothing but a sort of whirling emptiness.

"Willy, I can't do it!" she gasped, turning the chalk-white face upon him as the clapping began to diminish. "I just can't. I'm too scared."

"Aw, no, you ain't." Willy actually laughed. "You never been before."

But they'd never had such an audience before. However, there was no time to discuss it. The first staccato notes of the Golliwog's Cakewalk began: Willy gave her a gentle shove. And there she was: a blue gnome in a blue forest, dancing a grotesque and lonely little dance. That's all there was to it. The dance danced itself. *She*, Randy, just retired someplace and closed her eyes and put her fingers in her ears. Then the music was finished, she was making her little bow, the ocean of clapping was engulfing her, and Rush was grinning at her from the piano. Was it all over? Already? Why, it was too soon! Now she could hardly wait to dance again, and with eyes full of stars, ran up the back stairs, two at a time, to change her costume. Loving the world, she burst into the bedroom.

"Oh, you look beautiful, Mona!" gasped Randy; and Mona did look beautiful: a real fairy-tale princess in her dazzling robes. The wild hair, still not quite subdued, shone in a rebellious mass about her shoulders; and her cheeks were pink with excitement as well as rouge.

"You know, Randy," Mona said solemnly, as she put on her tall, gilt cardboard crown, "this is Life!" And Randy, ripping off the blue suit with its buttons popping, and glancing at the shimmering costume for her next dance, agreed with all her heart.

"H-m-m!" grunted Cuffy. "Tomorrow we'll have a powerful lot of cleaning up and dishwashing to do, don't forget. And that's life, too."

The play went marvelously well. Oliver forgot his lines only once, and there was hardly more than ten minutes' wait between scenes. Of course Rush's mustache fell off once, but he picked it up coolly and stuck it back in place without any embarrassment. And then during the saddest part of the play, when Glamorosa is imploring the witch Sourpuss to grant leniency to Prince Paragon, Willy's chirping shoe could be heard distinctly as he walked slowly

"YOU KNOW, RANDY, THIS IS LIFE!"

across the dining room behind the scenes. But otherwise, what a success! The applause they received would have warmed the heart of any producer in the world.

Afterward it was fun, too, when they came downstairs in their own clothes, traces of make-up still clinging to their faces, and mingled with the audience. What a lot of cookies they ate, now that their appetites had revived! And what a lot of compliments they got. Mrs. Oliphant embraced each of them warmly. Their cheeks were pressed against the icy links of her necklaces, and they breathed a scent of eau de Cologne and camphor. "It is the best performance you have given yet," she told them. Mr. and Mrs. Wheelwright were overwhelmed. They thought Mona ought to be in the movies, and Randy and Rush should be on the concert stage. Mr. and Mrs. Purvis thought so, too. The Melendy children felt that life would have been perfect if only they were allowed to give a new play every week.

The next day, as Cuffy had said, there was a lot of work to be done. Everyone seemed to be going someplace with a chair. The piano was to stay where it was until after Christmas because of family carol singing, but everything else had to go back in its place. Willy and Rush had to dismantle and store the scenery; and then clean and wax the floor. Randy and Mona washed endless sticky punch cups and glasses; endless dishes, and cooky plates and pitchers. But they did it willingly, standing side by side at the kitchen sink, and saying little. Each was lost in a golden haze of memory.

Every now and then one of them would break the silence with a rapt voice.

"They liked the part where Oliver trips over his sword, didn't they? Remember how they laughed?"

"It was wonderful!"

A little later: "The phosphorescent moon was a great success, don't you think? You could just hear them gasp."

"It was perfect!"

And before they knew it, before they even realized that they had been working for a long time, everything was washed and put away. The floor was mopped, the dishcloths rinsed and hung to dry beside the stove.

"It might interest you to know, ladies," said Rush, bursting through the swinging door, "it might just possibly interest you to know that Father and I have just counted the receipts and we find we're the possessors of twenty-six dollars and seventy-five cents!"

Twenty-six dollars and seventy-five cents! Almost enough to buy a bond and a half! It was a proud moment.

The next day after breakfast Father asked Mona to come into the study. He was quite formal about it, and Mona wondered if she had done anything wrong.

"Please sit down," said Father elegantly, motioning to a chair. She sat down and folded her hands. Father laughed. "Don't look so worried. You're not going to be scolded."

He picked up his special paperweight that was shaped like a lady's hand and examined it as though he had never seen it before.

"Mona," said Father at last, "you've really set your heart on being an actress, haven't you?"

"Of course, father." Mona looked surprised. About that there had never been any doubt. Not since the time

Mother had taken her to a matinee of *Peter Pan* when she was six.

"You know it's hard work, don't you? You know you have to be better than good at it or you might as well give up? You know you have to keep odd hours; work at night; sleep half the day; do the same thing, say the same words over and over and over again. Above all, you have to try to remain a real person in spite of all the imaginary people you are playing."

"Yes, father," said Mona automatically. What was all this leading to anyway? "I realize those things and I don't care. I still want to be an actress!"

Father nodded his head a little wearily.

"Yes, I know. You really mean it, don't you? All right then. How would you like to begin your career right now?"

"Now?" repeated Mona, bewildered. "Now? Father, what do you mean?"

"One of the people who came out with Mrs. Oliphant the day of the play is a radio director. He thinks he may have a part for you in one of his new radio serials. The part of a younger sister in a family play."

"You mean I'd be a professional? A real actress on the radio?" cried Mona.

"If you get the part," said Father. "You're to go to New York with Cuffy after New Year's and have an audition. If you make good you'll go in town twice a week for your broadcast. I believe the salary is quite generous."

"Oh, I'd do it free," Mona said. "I'd do it for nothing if they wanted me to."

"It won't be necessary. But one thing, Mona. You're very young to be doing this kind of work. *If* you make good, do you think I can count on you to keep your head? We don't want any junior prima donnas temperamenting around the house."

"Oh, father, I promise, I swear I won't be like that! I'll be good as an angel. I'll—I'll even darn Rush's socks without complaining. I'll play basketball at school; I'll wash all the stickiest, greasiest saucepans as if I loved it; I'll eat whole bales of spinach. I'll do anything. You'll see how good I'll be!"

"*If* you get the part," added Father.

But Mona knew she'd get the part. She went out of the study and out of the house. Her galoshes might have been thistledown; her coat might have been made of air; her feet didn't feel the earth beneath them, her hands didn't feel the surfaces they touched. She was in a state of bliss. Slowly, like a sleepwalker, she floated down to the brook. The pool above the falls was frozen solid: closed in a shell of clear black ice. Under it she could see the packed rows of little fish lying fast asleep. How beautiful they were!

"Oh, brook," said Mona aloud, in a quavery voice. "Oh, fish! I think I'm really going to be an actress at last!"

CHAPTER VIII

Noël, Noël

"THIS Christmas," Father said to them, "there is war; and I am poorer. You'll have to do a lot for yourselves. You'll have presents, of course, but perhaps not such fine ones as before. Try to remember how lucky we are. A family living together in a nice funny old house: a family that's fortunate enough to have light, and food, and warmth, and no fear of anything."

"That's quite a lot," Rush said afterward. "I've been reading the papers and I know that that's quite a lot for us to have."

So this year they made Christmas for themselves. And it was fun. More fun, really, than buying things ready-made. Willy and Rush investigated the woods and returned with a Christmas tree and a Yule log. With much prickling and ouching Randy and Mona made wreaths for the windows out of wild ground pine, evergreen, and holly. The old, scarred Christmas tree baubles were resurrected from their box, and in addition Oliver strung popcorn chains, and made many paste-blurred link chains of gold and silver paper; and there were bright woolen tassels of Mona's devising, sewn with Mrs. Oliphant's sparkling

THE HANDSOMEST TREE THEY'D EVER HAD

sequins. The tree was beautiful when it was trimmed: the handsomest tree they'd ever had, the Melendys thought.

Christmas looked promising in spite of what Father had said. An enormous box had arrived from Mrs. Oliphant; and Oliver happened to know that there were other mysterious boxes on the top shelf of the linen closet. Cuffy spent the day before Christmas locked in the kitchen; nobody was even allowed to look in at the windows. A dazzling fragrance breathed itself through the crack under the door, and filled the whole house with frankincense and myrrh.

This year the children had made most of their presents. Mona had knitted scarves for everyone out of the most brilliant colors she could find; they were like woolen rainbows. Randy had made a big sachet for Mona, and another for Mrs. Oliphant; a pincushion (stuffed with milkweed) for Cuffy; a blotter holder for Father's desk; and for Oliver she'd filled a scrapbook with cutout pictures of planes, battleships, submarines, and tanks. For Rush she had saved enough out of her allowances to buy a record he'd wanted for a long time: boys are so hard to make things for, and she wanted to give him something he'd really like.

Rush had composed a piece of music for everyone. A sonata for Father, called "Opus I." A sonata for Mrs. Oliphant, called "Opus II." The rest of them had regular names: Cuffy's was called "Music to Cook By"; Mona's was "Incidental Music for *Macbeth*"; Randy's was "Funeral March in F" (she loved funeral marches); and Oliver's was a "Military March" which he didn't appreciate. To Willy, who had often displayed a wistful interest in music, Rush gave a recorder and some easy tunes to play on it. Thereafter mournful tootlings could be heard coming faintly from the stable at odd hours of the day or night when Willy wasn't working.

Oliver made thick, wobbly, clay ash trays for everyone, though nobody smoked except Father. "They can use 'em for pins and elastic bands and things," Oliver told himself comfortably.

To compensate for the humbleness of their gifts they took great pains with the wrappings. Especially Mona, who spent literally days rustling and crackling about among crepe and tissue papers, and was always trailing bits of string and red ribbon.

"Sh-h-h," Rush said to Randy. "Don't tell anybody, but I think she's building a nest."

On Christmas Eve they sang carols, all standing around the piano in the living room. The tree glittered dimly in its shadowed corner: it was asleep, waiting; and under its protecting boughs it hid a rich harvest of unopened presents. Oliver's sock hung empty from the mantel (the rest of them had given up stockings this Christmas) and the Yule log in the fireplace was waiting for tomorrow, too.

They sang "God Rest Ye Merry, Gentlemen" and "Silent Night" and "Adeste Fideles" and "Oh, Little Town of Bethlehem," and "Noël, Noël," and lots of others. Randy's favorite was "We Three Kings of Orient Are." As she sang its minor air she could almost see the three kings riding on three tall camels: their glorious robes and glorious gifts all silvered and dazzling under the light of the Star.

"Look!" cried Mona, when they had finished. "It's snowing!"

How perfect! Snow on Christmas Eve. Please, please, let it last until tomorrow!

When she was ready for bed Randy leaned out the window. Far out, so that she could feel the little cold sharp flakes against her cheek. They glittered like tinsel in the light from the window. She could hear the brook murmuring under the ice, and the spruce branches sighing and sighing under the snow.

> "Si-ilent night,
> Ho-oly night,"

Randy sang in an exalted voice; and Cuffy pulled her in by the back of her pajamas.

"You want to catch your death? Pile into bed now, it's almost nine."

Randy threw her arms around Cuffy's neck. "Oh, I love Christmas Eve!" she cried. "Even better than Christmas I love it. Because everything's just about to happen!"

"Influenza's about to happen if you don't get into bed with them windows open," growled Cuffy, giving her a kiss and a shove both at once.

Randy went to bed but not to sleep. For a long time she lay listening to the cold whisper of the snow. "Christmas, Christmas, Christmas," it was saying. She couldn't help wishing that she believed in Santa Claus again. On such a night as this one could almost hear sleigh bells in the sky.

It had just got over being dark when she woke up: the morning was still new and unspoiled, like a pool into which no one has thrown a pebble. The first thing she saw was a big white cuff of snow on the window sill. She got up and looked out. The floor was ice under her bare soles but she preferred the discomfort to the boredom of putting on bedroom slippers; she gathered a handful of snow from the sill and stood there licking it thoughtfully and looking out the window at Christmas Day. A few flakes still fell, but whether from the sky or from lightly moving branches it was hard to tell. The trees stood up out of the whiteness, black as ebony, and fine as lace. It was like the snow and trees that a man named Peter Breughel used to paint. Mrs. Oliphant had a book full of his pictures. At the thought of Mrs. Oliphant she remembered the mysterious box downstairs; she remembered Christmas and the presents, and was very happy.

But, oh, it was cold! All of a sudden a shiver crawled over her, beginning under her insteps and traveling right up over her scalp. Randy banged the window shut and leaped into her warm bed. She didn't stay there long, though. Soon she was up again, and properly robed and slippered, opened the door into the hall. The house was warm and still. I am the only one awake, thought Randy.

Or was she?

There was a faint chink, and a shuffle, and the next thing she saw was Oliver coming slowly up the stairs in his bare feet, exploring a bulging sock as he came. His hair was standing straight up on one side like the feathers of a young thrush.

"Merry Christmas," whispered Randy. "Where are your slippers?"

"Merry Christmas," replied Oliver. "I don't need them."

"Look, Randy, I've got a flashlight," he said. "A pocket one, and two little tanks, and there's something here that feels like a hand grenade." But it turned out to be a baseball.

For breakfast that morning they had waffles and country sausage, and hot chocolate with big lumps of whipped cream on top, just like restaurant hot chocolate. Afterward Rush went into the living room and played the Mendelssohn Wedding March, because it was the first thing he thought of, and Father threw open the doors, and there was the lighted Christmas tree, come into its own at last: a shimmering mirage, a tree of Paradise, a pyramid of jewels.

Father distributed the presents. Papers flew, strings were tossed aside. Oliver grew white and strained with excitement: probably he would be sick at his stomach when this was over.

All the presents were successful. Cuffy had made taffy apples, and boxes of fudge, and gingerbread men for everyone. She even had a beef bone all done up in tissue paper for Isaac. Father's present was swell new books: lots of books, and all the kinds they liked best. In addition he gave Rush a book of records: the Mozart Piano Concerto in C minor. Mona got the musical powder box she had craved for so long; Randy, a whole stack of drawing paper, and a really super paintbox; Oliver, a Meccano set; and Isaac, a new red collar with his name on it.

"I thought you said we weren't going to have such good

presents this year!" said Rush, looking accusingly at Father.

"I'm glad if you like them. But just wait till you see what Mrs. O has sent!" Father replied.

Her box was the last one. Mona cut the string, Randy pulled off the paper, Rush pried open the lid, and Oliver dived in. Inside there were four pairs of ice skates! Ice skates with shoes attached to them; just the right size for each child. "Oh, boy!" said Rush and Oliver. "Gee *whiz!*" said Randy. "How absolutely divine!" said Mona.

Besides the skates there was a new, a brand, glistening-new typewriter for Father, a quilted bathrobe for Cuffy, a big warm sweater for Willy, and a little warm sweater for Isaac!

And just as they were beginning to settle down, and had all the strings and ribbons curled up in a box and all the paper folded into a neat pile for Randy's paper salvage, the front doorbell rang! When they got to the door they were just in time to see the back of a pickup truck vanishing over the hill.

"Now, who do you suppose—what's *that?*" cried Cuffy, looking down.

There was a long coffin-shaped box on the front doorstep, with perforations in the lid.

"Maybe somebody's left a baby for us to take care of," said Randy hopefully. "See, there's a card under that red ribbon bow on the top." They looked at the card. It said:

Merry Christmas Folks
from
Mr. and Mrs. Ed J. Wheelwright

P.S. Handle with care, especially when opening

They were very careful: the same suspicion was forming in every mind. And it turned out to be correct. For when they removed the lid, there, nestled in a burlap sack, was Crusty Wheelwright, the alligator, smiling his dreamy and hypocritical smile.

Father just said "Well!" and leaned against the door-jamb for support. Oliver and Rush and Willy were delighted. Randy was pleased in a dubious sort of way, Mona shrank back with an affected little squeal, and Cuffy said (and repeated it several times a day for the next week or so), "My lands! Some people sure know how to pass the buck!" She was quite cross, too, when Oliver said, "Oh, boy, hip, hip, hooray! Now we can keep him in our bathtub!"

Needless to say, this did not transpire. In a day or two Willy got a tank built for Crusty which they kept in the furnace room. But in the meanwhile his abode was a laundry tub in the kitchen. It was an uneasy period for Cuffy.

"Some Christmas," remarked Rush in a satisfied tone at the end of the day. He was playing Randy's Funeral March for her, very quietly in the dusk. "I bet we're just about the only kids in the county, maybe even the whole state, that got such a big live alligator for a Christmas present."

"Or maybe the whole country, or maybe an alligator at all," agreed Randy, nodding her head slowly. "Yes. You know, Rush, it's funny, but we always did seem to be luckier than most of the people we know."

CHAPTER IX

The Light in the Woods

AFTER New Year's a strange and fascinating life began for Mona. One day she went to New York with Cuffy, wearing her best dress, her charm bracelet, and some new shoes with the beginnings of heels. Randy hugged her and said, "I know you'll be wonderful!" Rush said, "You go ahead and knock 'em cold, Mona; I've got my fingers crossed." Oliver didn't say anything: he hung back and looked at her as if she were a stranger, and then, suddenly, just as she was leaving he smiled at her: his new, guileless smile with two teeth missing in the front. Mona hugged them all, feeling grateful and loving.

All the way in on the train she kept thinking about them. I must do well, she thought; I want them to be proud of me.

Cuffy was the only one who had stage fright. Her face was pink, and her breath came fast. She kept looking at her watch, putting on and taking off her gloves, and when they arrived at the vast New York office building which was their destination she gave the taxi driver five dollars and would have gone off without the change if Mona hadn't reminded her.

"Don't feel sick or anything, do you?" Cuffy demanded anxiously as they went up in the elevator. "Wouldn't like some spirits of ammonia, would you? There's nothing to be nervous about, you know."

"*I'm* not nervous, Cuffy," Mona said, smiling at her.

At the twenty-seventh floor they entered the office of a Mr. Gage Protheroe; an important gentleman to judge from the number of stenographers, messenger boys, and unexplained people with papers in their hands who were hovering about him. Mona remembered him from the day of the show.

"Ah, yes, little lady!" Mr. Protheroe exclaimed, breaking away from the knot of people. "Come right along, come right along. This is Mr. Niles Carrington, the director of *The Penfold People*. Niles, this little lady, we hope, is to take June Palfrey's place as Polly Penfold."

Mr. Carrington had a flap of heavy hair on his brow; and his shirt was open at the collar. He looked at Mona exactly as he might have looked at a pair of shoes he was thinking of buying.

"She seems sort of young," he said at last. "June is sixteen, after all. Think this one can handle it?"

My, was Cuffy ever mad! She positively crackled with indignation. "She can handle anything!" said Cuffy. "I never saw such a young one for acting. You'll find out."

Mr. Carrington smiled at that. "Okay, I'll find out. By the way, what's her name?"

"Mona Melendy," volunteered Mona, tired of being referred to as though she weren't there.

"That's a pretty good name," Mr. Carrington decided.

"Distinctive. We won't have to change it to Jennifer This or Sandra That. It's a pretty good name."

"Thank you," said Mona.

All this time they had been walking down a long corridor, and now Mr. Protheroe held open a door and they all went into a broadcasting studio. It was a small, electrically lighted room with a microphone in the middle of it, and some hard chairs, and a piano. Set in the wall was a large plate-glass window which revealed various mysterious instruments, and a pale-faced man wearing spectacles who looked solemnly out at them like a fish in an aquarium.

"All right, little lady," said Mr. Protheroe. "Here's a script. Let's see what you can do with it. Stand close to the mike."

Mona read the script aloud. It required everything of her. It required her to be happy, to be sad, to laugh, cry, scream with terror, and moan with pain; but she didn't feel that it was too severe a test. She was sustained by the familiar sense of belief in her own power which always accompanied her acting.

"Now again," commanded Mr. Carrington, when she had finished.

All in all she read the script four times. Other people were called in to listen and confer; and at the end of it Mr. Protheroe said, "All right, little lady. I think you'll do." And she overheard Mr. Carrington saying to Cuffy, "I guess you're right. She seems to be able to handle almost anything."

On Tuesdays and Fridays she was to go to town with Cuffy: an hour of rehearsal with the other actors first, and then the performance itself at four o'clock. She had special permission to miss half a day at school twice a week, though she would have to make it up later.

On the day of her first performance Father took a day off and went to the broadcasting studio with Mona. The rest of the family listened in at home.

"My heart's thumping like anything," Randy said, swallowing. "And the palms of my hands are wet. I feel just like I did the day of the show."

"You can count on it Mona's not feeling like that, though." Cuffy shook her head admiringly. "When I took her up for the audition I was trembling like a blancmange, but *she* was just as cool as a cucumber."

A silvery peal sounded from the radio. "It's four o'clock!" said Rush excitedly. "She'll be coming on in a minute. Listen!"

There was a moment of stillness, then a faint sound like a sigh, and a man's voice began to speak. It was a rich, velvety voice: you could almost hear the nap on it, Rush thought. "Good afternoon, ladies and gentlemen," it said. "Do you suffer from indigestion? Are you a victim of heartburn, nausea, irritation after eating? Do you look longingly at foods you dare not touch? Toss feverishly all night after a hearty dinner? Ladies and gentlemen, there is an answer, a remedy for your problems. It is an old one, a reliable one: and in all probability one which your mother, yes, even your grandmother, used with beneficial results. What is its name? Aqualixir! Just ask for the little green package at any drugstore."

"Mona Melendy, the Princess of the Pancreas," said Rush. But the voice was continuing.

"This afternoon, ladies and gentlemen, we present

another chapter in the lives of the fascinating Penfold family. Added to today's performance is a surprise in the form of a new little lady who is to play the part of Polly Penfold, fourteen-year-old sister of Diana, Bob, and Jimmy. She is little Miss Mona Melendy, blonde, blue-eyed, pretty as a picture. I just wish you could see her, ladies and gentlemen; I know you would give her a great big hand. And now, THE PENFOLD PEOPLE!"

"Boy, she'll never be the same again," said Rush, but Cuffy sh-h-h-ed him indignantly, and the play began. There was a lot of talk at first between some young lady and a man who seemed to want to marry her.

"Sister Diana and a swain, I guess," said Rush sourly. "All this love stuff gives me a pain."

"Oh, Barry. I—I just *wish* you'd stop talking about it," pleaded the young woman tearfully. "You know there's no one else to take care of them now that Daddy's gone away. They need me so."

"Now, Diana [It was Mona's voice], you know that's all nonsense. We can look after ourselves perfectly well."

"Polly! You've been eavesdropping! Where were you?"

"Oh, I was just sitting under the piano sort of thinking."

And so it went; a whole half hour of it.

"Gee, she sounded swell," Rush pronounced at the end. "It's a pretty hammy program, I'd say, but she's good. I just hope she doesn't get stuck up, that's all."

"She won't. Mona's wonderful!" said Randy fervently.

Cuffy was so overcome that they actually caught her in the act of mopping her eyes with a handkerchief.

"Why, *Cuffy!*" cried Randy. "I never knew you were so sentimental."

The days went by. Mona's broadcast became an accepted part of the routine of their lives. Her picture appeared in newspapers every now and then, and after a week or two she even began getting fan letters! Randy and Rush (especially Rush) watched her like hawks for the first sign of temperament. But apparently there was no temperament. Mona was blissfully happy and kept her word to Father: she darned Rush's socks, ate spinach, went out for basketball, and performed with grace all the duties which were loathsome to her.

On the contrary, toward the end of January, it was Rush who seemed to be indulging in fits of temperament. After school he lurked about indoors and snapped at anyone who suggested going out. When his music went wrong, he crashed his fists down on the keys and slammed the piano lid shut. He wouldn't eat enough, and spent useless hours lying on the floor listening to the radio.

"Come on out, Rush," begged Randy one day after school. "It's a wonderful day and Isaac needs a good run; he's getting as fat as a pig."

"I don't feel like it," replied Rush ungraciously.

"Ah, please! Mona's still at school, making up for Tuesday, and Oliver's got to stay in on account of his cold. I don't feel like playing all alone."

"So what? I don't feel like going out."

"I wish you would. We could go for a ride on our bikes. And you ought to: you look like a potato sprout from moping indoors all the time."

Rush turned on her furiously. "Will you please, for Pete's sake, get out of here and mind your own business?

If I want to mope, I'll mope, and neither you nor anybody else can do a thing about it. This is one country that's still free."

"What's the matter with you, Rush?" Randy was almost in tears. "For two weeks now you've been just as cross as a bear. You snap at everybody all the time. Gee whiz, you never used to be like that; I mean we quarreled sometimes, everybody does, but mostly you were always swell."

Rush glowered and kicked the piano stool. He hated like poison to apologize for things, but he knew just as well as anybody else what a beast he was being, and Randy was a good kid. She deserved an explanation.

"Well, I guess it's like this, Ran." Rush cleared his throat, pushed his hands into his pockets, and clenched his fists. "It's kind of hard to say. I mean it's about Mona, and you'll think I'm a heel. It's not that I'm jealous, exactly. Or maybe I am in a way, but not just because of all the glory she's getting. No. I mean, gee, here I am a guy thirteen years old: the eldest son of the Melendy family, et cetera, and what am I doing to help swell finances? Nothing, that's what. And here my sister, only a year and a half older, is able to buy Defense Stamps like chewing gum, and add to the family exchequer besides. If I could just do *something!*"

"But why can't you?" Randy said.

"Tell me what! I've been racking my brains, of course, what do you suppose? But I can't think of a thing. Grover Pettybone has the Carthage paper route, and he's so old I wouldn't want to give him any competition. I could sell magazine subscriptions, maybe, but look at the population of Carthage! I'd be lucky if I sold a dozen, including the ones Father and Cuffy'd think they'd have to buy. I could shovel off snow, or mow lawns, or work in gardens, but this is the sticks, and most everybody lives on his own land and uses his own family instead of hired hands. No, I tell you it's a problem!"

"I can think of something," Randy said slowly. "But you won't like it."

"What is it? Why not?"

"You could give piano lessons," said Randy firmly.

"Wh-a-a-t? You're nuts!"

"Now don't be like that, Rush. You know as well as I do that there hasn't been a music teacher for miles around, ever since the last one got married and moved to Hartford. Mrs. Wheelwright told you that the same time she told me. And she told us that Judge Laramy was mad as hops 'cause she'd talked him into buying a piano so Floyd and Myrtle could learn to play. And then right after he got it, she went and eloped."

"Well, what's that—"

"Now wait. I know of three other families that have pianos just standing around going sour. And the one in the school gym. Nobody ever plays that except Melva Jenks, and all she ever plays is 'My Rosary.' I bet you could get more pupils than you could take care of in no time at all. You're good too. You know you are. Remember how you outgrew that teacher in New York, and how even Mr. Dohansky said you were a project—progeny, or whatever it is."

"Prodigy," Rush corrected her. "Well, sure. But if you think I'm going to waste my youth trying to pound music into a goon like Floyd Laramy, you're crazy."

"All right," said Randy, sweeping out of the room. "I thought you really wanted a job. But I guess it was just talk as usual, that's all."

"Listen, you stop being Cuffy," Rush called after her; but left alone, he went over to the piano. Standing, he touched the keys with his left hand: a warm chord came to life and hung, slowly, diminishing on the air. Yes, he was good, all right. I'd be a dope if I didn't know that, he thought. He sat down on the piano bench, and under his fingers the music began to grow, up and out, tall and wide: a tree of sound, springing from strong, orderly roots.

Maybe she's right, thought Rush against the music. I guess I could do it. The picture of Floyd Laramy's broad, unsmiling face floated across his mind. Floyd Laramy who enjoyed two things, eating and fighting, and who thought Rush was a sissy because he knew about music and liked mathematics. Rush sighed and closed the piano lid. "I guess I could do it. But, boy, at what a cost."

This is a day of sacrifices, Rush told himself. In wartime everybody makes sacrifices. But that was just a lot of words: he might as well have been saying one, two, three, the cat ran up the tree. All he knew was that he wanted to do something. He wanted to help: his family and, in a way, his country. "Let's see if I've got a little gold halo shining around my head," Rush said aloud and went and looked in a mirror. But he hadn't.

That is how it came to pass that on the bulletin board at school the next day there was a little card saying: "Piano lessons. 50 cents an hour. Rush Melendy."

Mr. Coughing, the principal, helped. He spoke to Judge Laramy who spoke (firmly) to Floyd and Myrtle. He also mentioned the matter to the half dozen other parents who had pianos as well as children, and in a week's time Rush had eight pupils: one every day after school and three on Saturdays. Each day, besides his schoolbooks, he carried a brief case with music in it, and finger exercises, and lined music paper.

February was very cold. There was what Willy (who really knew nothing about it) called a "black frost." The brook froze over solid. Even the little cascade was covered with a deep, ruffly collar of ice, although underneath it you could still hear the water tinkling and rushing. After school each day they tried out Mrs. Oliphant's ice skates. They could hardly wait to get back in the afternoons, flinging their books down on the hall table, searching for their skates, not even removing their mittens as they snatched a quick cooky from the jar in the pantry. For the next hour or two, until it was really dark, their part of the valley was filled with the sound of voices, bumps, outcries, and the peculiar ringing strokes of blades on ice.

Mona and Rush had had the most practice. They spiraled about on the glossy surface, falling very seldom. Randy fell a lot. She would seem to be getting the hang of it, to be skimming like a bird over the cold, black mirror, and then, slam, just as she was breathing naturally and trying not to wave her arms, down she would go! In a sitting position most frequently, but often on her face, her side, the back of her head. All the places where her bones met in corners, like knees and elbows, were bruised and sore. But the cold held, the ice became even stronger, and her persistence triumphed; at last she was almost as good as Mona herself.

Oliver just walked on his skates, taking each one completely off the ice before he set it down again. He walked with a strange, jerky gait, keeping close to the banks, his arms flapping like wings, and his mittened fists grasping at twigs, branches, passers-by, and anything to balance himself; he fell on an average of once every three minutes. He didn't smile or speak; his eyes were set in a stare of glassy intensity, his tongue stuck out at the corner of his mouth, and from time to time he made a small grunting sound of effort. Oliver took skating hard, and refused to be helped.

One Friday when the brook had been frozen for more than a week, Rush said, "We're all pretty good now. What do you say we go exploring down the brook and see where it takes us? When we come to rough places or holes or open water, we can make our way along the banks."

"Why, you know perfectly well we'll just end up in Carthage," Mona said.

"The other way, then, why not? We've never gone very far in that direction, even walking, the woods are so thick," Randy suggested.

"All right. You want to come along, Oliver?"

"Huh?" said Oliver, who hadn't heard a word. "I don't want to go anywhere. I'm busy working." Which was true. Nobody could have called Oliver's method of skating a pleasure.

They had to walk down the banks at the side of the frozen cascade, and then they took to the brook again. It was dangerous and eventful skating: boulders kept rearing up from the ice, and there were twigs and snags of dead branches sticking out like antlers to trip one, and live twigs and branches reaching down from above to slap one's face and pull one's hair. Expertly Mona curved and dipped and dodged. Randy toiled along painfully in the rear, and Rush, bless him, would skim ahead and then come swooping back with words of comfort and encouragement.

"Come on, Sonja Henie," he'd call cheerfully. "Look out for that air hole. You're doing swell."

It was all woods on both sides. Thick, thick, noiseless woods. I wish I could look at 'em, thought Randy, eyes glued to the ice under her feet. This way I'll never know where I've been.

"Want to rest awhile?" asked Rush, returning. "Whew, I'm hot, and you're brick-red yourself."

"It's from holding my breath," explained Randy, sinking gratefully down on the cushion of dry snow and dead leaves that covered the bank. Rush sat down beside her and took off his knitted cap. His curly hair was damp from heat, but his breath came out in a little white frosty cloud.

"Boy, have I ever had a day," said he.

"My ankles hurt," said Randy. "Why? What happened to you?"

"Well, you know Floyd Laramy?"

"Yes, worse luck. What's he done now?"

"Today was his lesson day. Gee, Randy, it's been tough. Everybody else, all the other kids, are swell. I think they like studying with me because I'm a kid myself. Some of them are kind of dumb, but they're all swell, and Steve Ladislas is even going to be pretty good someday if he works. But that Laramy guy! You know what he does? He pretends he's deaf, and whenever I tell him anything he says 'I beg your pardon? I didn't quite catch it.' And kind of grins in a nasty way. He's had five lessons now and he still doesn't know an eighth note from his own shoe, and he can hardly play the C major scale. So today I went in right after school. Boy, is that piano a beauty, you could play Chopsticks on it and it would sound like the Chromatic Fantasy, but it's just being wasted. First thing that happened was that I sat on the bench by Floyd and he slammed the piano lid down on my knuckles. Look." Rush took off a mitten and showed Randy his bruised fingers.

"The pig!" said Randy warmly. "What did you do?"

"Oh, he pretended it was an accident, said he was sorry and all that. But I saw through him. Next thing he kept knocking the music off the rack, and I kept picking it up, like a dope, and saying 'Now look, Floyd. This is a whole note. See? It's round like a doughnut.' And so on, and so on. And then I say, 'Now play me the G major scale very slowly.' And what does he do? He lies down, just lies down on the floor and says, 'Ho hum, am I ever fatigued. Doesn't this beastly grind get you down, old boy?' He's making me look like a sissy, see, because I'm giving music lessons. So I say, 'Cut the comedy, drip, and play me the G major scale;' and he gets up and says, 'Make me,' and so I say, 'Okay, I'll make you,' and, uh, I-uh, well, Ran, I *socked* him."

"Oh, Rush, you *didn't!* And his father's a judge!"

"I know; that's what I thought, too. So I went right to his study and knocked; and when he said 'Come in,' I said, 'Judge Laramy, I just socked your son; I socked him pretty hard. I'm sorry but I couldn't help it. So now I want to refund the two dollars you've paid me so far, because Floyd doesn't want to take piano, and I guess I can't teach him.' "

"What did he ever say?"

"He said, 'Son, I paid more'n a thousand dollars for that piano two years ago. Floyd and Myrtle are going to learn to play it! If socking is included in your technique of education, well, that's none of my business as long as they really learn. You come back here next week. I'll have a little talk with Floyd in the meantime, and you forget about refunding the money.' "

"Why, he sounds kind of nice," said Randy, staggering to her feet. "That cross-looking man, with those eyebrows that look like two live mice! I'm scared of him."

"He was nice," Rush agreed, steering her away from a rock. "But I felt awful about it anyway."

"Yoo-hoo," came Mona's echoing voice from far ahead among the trees.

"Yoo-hoodle-oodle-oo," they yodeled in answer, and quickened their gliding.

"It's getting kind of dark," observed Randy; "maybe we ought to turn around."

"Oh, pretty soon. And guess what, Ran, a good thing happened, too. I met Mr. Cotton, the Methodist minister, on the street today. He told me Simon Turner's been called into the army. So he's minus an organist. He thought maybe I could take the job."

"Rush, how marvelous! But you don't know how to play an organ, do you?"

"His is only an old-fashioned melodeon. I've fooled around with the Wheelwrights' plenty and I can play it fine. They told him about me. He says he'll give me five dollars a week."

"*Five dollars!*" exclaimed Randy. "This is going to be a wealthy family."

High in the pale-green sky the evening star was hanging, solitary and pure. Mona called again, and her voice had the faraway, remembered sound of voices heard at dusk. Rush let go of Randy's arm. "I'm just going on ahead a minute to see where she is. I'll be right back."

Randy struggled on by herself. Her ankles were so tired and aching that she could hardly keep her balance, and when, in the half-darkness, she collided with a dead branch, her skate caught and she fell hard.

"Ouch," said Randy out loud. "*Ow-ooo!*"

Tears of pain came into her eyes, and she sat up, rocking to and fro, and holding her ankle. "Rush!" wailed Randy. "Oh, Mona, come back, I've hurt myself!"

She kept on calling until Mona came gliding out of the dusk like a ghost in ski pants.

"Now, Randy, not *again!* You can't always be hurting yourself in inconvenient places like this. Stand up. You're all right."

Randy tried to stand up, but immediately sat down again and began to cry in good earnest. "My ankle," she wept. "It hurts, hurts, hurts."

"That's all right, Ran," said Rush, appearing suddenly at Mona's side. "You just bawl all you want to and pretty soon it'll feel better. And don't worry, we'll get you home somehow."

"But how?" whispered Mona under cover of Randy's sobs. Aloud she said, "Rush, give me your scarf, it's the largest one. I know a bandage for a sprained ankle. Look, Randy darling, I'm going to take your skate off and do up your ankle and then it'll feel much better."

The funny thing was that it did. The pain abated almost miraculously as soon as Mona had bound the ankle up snugly in Rush's scarf. Randy's sobs grew less, resolved themselves into an occasional gasp and sniffle, and wiping her tears with her mitten, she smiled gratefully at Mona.

"*I* took first aid, if you remember, Rush," Mona couldn't resist saying.

Her brother nodded sheepishly. "They laughed when I sat down at the piano," he said.

"Well, we can't leave her here to freeze, and it's getting darker by the minute. If only we didn't have these skates on we could sort of carry her."

"Maybe I'd better skate back and get Willy," suggested Rush. "Only how would *he* get her home?"

"Look," said Randy suddenly, "I see a light!" They turned and stared. Sure enough shining among the branches far back in the woods there was a light.

"It's a house," Rush said. "I'll go. You stay with Randy."

Feeling rather brave he hobbled off on his skates in the direction of the light. It was nearly dark, now, but fortunately the snow gave a sort of radiance to the earth so that he could see where he was going fairly well. It was very uncomfortable to be walking on skate blades over rough ground. Rush fell once or twice himself, and thought, all we need is for me to sprain my ankle now. The woods were full of shadows, and ominous stillness, and the light was farther away than it had seemed. But at last he came to a clearing and there in the middle of it sat a low, wooden house.

It was comfortably settled between bare lilac bushes as high as the roof, and the winter skeleton of a vine clung to its grey clapboards in a pattern like feather stitching. The encroaching woods were kept at bay by a narrow picket fence, and a vast tidy bulwark of stacked logs. Smoke was rising out of the chimney on the evening air, Rush could smell it, and in one window a light was burning: an old-fashioned kerosene lamp with a cracked green shade. Beyond the lamp somebody was moving to and fro.

Rush went up to the door, knocked, and listened. He could hear an old voice saying, "Go see who 'tis, Will, and don't let Spooky get out."

There was a shuffle, shuffle, shuffle and the door opened releasing a smell of cooking that Rush even in his haste and anxiety took note of. A tall old man with a beard was looking down at him.

"What's matter, sonny? You lost?"

Rush explained.

"Why, I'll come down and help you. We'll bring her back here and you can phone your folks. Say-rah," he called, and a spare old lady appeared in the door. "I'm going out a minnit. Little girl down to the crick, sprained her ankle skating. Where's my boots?"

In a minute he and Rush (wearing borrowed boots) were making their way among the trees, the old man carrying a lantern.

"This is awfully kind of you, sir," Rush said in his best manner; the one that nobody but strangers ever heard.

"Oh, 'tain't nothing, sonny. What's your name? I'm Will Pepper."

Before Rush had a chance to reply they had reached the brook. Mona and Randy looked up at them, blinking like two little owls in the light.

"Well, well, sister, ya sure fixed yerself up this time, didn't you? Take the lantern, will you, sonny? Now. Easy does it. There we are." And he had picked Randy up in his arms and was starting back towards the house.

"Isn't she too heavy for you, sir?" said Rush.

"Heavy? Why, she don't weigh no more than a kitten, do you, sister? Must be most frozen, ain't ya? When we get up to the house, my wife will give you a cup of tea to cheer you up."

Rush led the way with the lantern, and Mona brought up the rear, tottering on her skate blades like a Manchu lady with bound feet. When they came to the house the skates and Rush's borrowed boots were left outside and they entered quietly, padding in woolen socks.

Mrs. Pepper was tiny, bent with age and rheumatism, and her knuckles were gnarled and swollen; but yet her step was light, almost tripping, and quick as a girl's. She fussed over Randy, and gave them all big cups of strong tea. The Melendys sipped the forbidden adult drink with a sort of guilty relish.

Randy lay on a little hard couch with Spooky the cat beside her and a multicolored crocheted afghan over her. She looked about the room. It was bare and scrubbed and clean; the walls were white, and lined with long cracks like wrinkles of character in an old face. She liked the huge black stove that dominated the place; and the pots and pans all hanging neatly from their hooks, and the shelves of blue willowware. On the table was a red-checked cloth that had been darned often, and on the wall there was a very nice picture of a little girl trying on a pair of spectacles. Underneath the picture it said: "Now they'll think I'm Gwandma!"

The telephone bloomed out of the wall like a kind of robot morning-glory. When Rush picked up the receiver he heard a voice in the middle of a conversation "—she was over to the Social last night. I didn't think she looked very good. After all she ain't sixteen years old any more, and pale-pink taffeta with ruffles don't look so good—"

Rush hung up hastily. "There's someone on the line."

"That's Harriet Widdicorn," remarked Mrs. Pepper. "This is a party line, but there's nobody else gets a chance at it. Harriet's an awful busy talker. Makes a lifework of it, you might say. We never pick up the receiver that her voice isn't inside of it, buzzing away, buzzing away, just like a hornet."

After Rush had tried three times and the voice was still talking, Mr. Pepper strode across the room, took the receiver from his hand and spoke into the phone. "That's enough, Harriet, you ought to keep something back for later. We've got an emergency down here; little girl's had an accident on ice skates."

"She loves accidents," whispered Mrs. Pepper. "Talk and other folks' bad luck is all she lives for."

Rush finally got Father on the telephone; repeated to him the directions Mr. Pepper gave him, and Father said he'd come right over in the Motor.

"So you're from over't the Four-Story Mistake, are

you?" Mr. Pepper inquired. "The old Cassidy house, eh? Why, I know that place real well. Used to play cowboys and Indians all over the grounds with the Cassidy boys fifty-sixty years ago."

"You say you knew the Cassidy family, Mr. Pepper?" Mona set her teacup down abruptly.

"Sure did. Knew 'em real well. We both did, didn't we, Say-rah? Went to school with some of 'em. They was a real big family. Lively, too."

"Was one of the daughters named Clarinda, by any chance?"

"Clarinda? Yes, indeed. I remember her real good, though she was quite some older than the rest of us. She didn't live there so long, either."

"What happened to her? Did she get married?"

"Her? No, at least not when we knew her. She ran away from home. She had a lot of spunk."

The Melendys' ears pricked up like rabbits'. "Ran away? Whatever for?"

"Well, seems she wanted to go on the stage, or some such. I don't just recall."

"Pshaw, I do," said Mrs. Pepper, closing the oven door smartly. "She wanted to be a dancer. One of them fancy dancers, you know. And what's more she got to be one, too, and was real famous in her day."

Randy sat up suddenly.

"A dancer? Please tell about it," she begged.

"Well, near's I recall she was about sixteen or seventeen when the family moved here. That was back—let's see, Will, when was that?"

"Oh, '73 or '74, I guess. Mighty long ago anyways."

"1871," said Mona firmly. It sounded just as distant as 1492 to her.

"That's right, 'bout then. Before that they'd been living in Europe. Paris, France, and Rome, Italy, and places like that. Clarinda she was the oldest girl and her papa's pet and all, so she got to go to operas and theayters and places where she saw them ballet dancers. Nothing would satisfy her but she must learn to dance. Nobody approved of it, but her papa was awful fond of her and finally she wore him down and he got a dancing teacher to come to the hotel every day and give her lessons. A couple of years that went on; but when she let on she'd like to make a career of it her papa hit the ceiling and told her she was never, never to dance again. I guess that's really why they packed up and came home even before they intended to."

"Did you ever see her dance?"

"Just once, and I never forgot it. She danced for me and another little girl named Ottilie Schmidt. She took us up to her room one day; seems to me it was way up in the attic somewheres. On account of the builder leaving off a floor, and all, they had to use what space they had."

The Melendys exchanged a significant glance.

"Well, so she locked the door and she says to Ottilie and me, 'Don't you dare tell Papa, cross your hearts. He hates for me to dance.' And we crossed our hearts and promised. So then she got a pair of dancing slippers out of a box under her bed and she took off her heavy skirt and danced in her petticoat. My, she was graceful! Right up on the tips of her toes, she went; to and fro and to and fro, twirling around and jumping way up in the air, and

SHE DANCED IN HER PETTICOAT

coming down so light the pitcher didn't even rattle in the washbasin. Ottilie and me, we just sat there with our mouths open, and our thick-soled boots out on the floor in front of us, feeling as slow and heavy as two little heifers."

"What did she look like?"

"She was a real handsome young lady," Mr. Pepper volunteered. "Lots of dark curly hair, and the littlest waist!"

"Whatever happened to her?"

"One night she disappeared. Just disappeared. The next morning they found a rope made out of sheets a-hanging from her winda; and there was a note on her pilla saying she was gone forever. Gone to be a dancer, the note said."

"Oh, her papa was wild, poor man. He raised heaven and earth to get her back. But she wouldn't come back, and there wasn't nobody could find her. She'd just disappeared. At least Clarinda Cassidy had disappeared: a new young lady with a furrin name rose up in her place and got to be a real famous ballet dancer."

"What was her name?"

"I was worried you was going to ask me that. Anastasia was the first name, wasn't it, Will? But what was the last?"

"Well, 'twasn't Bulova, 'cause that's the watch. And 'twasn't Popova, 'cause that's the muffin. 'Twas something kinda like 'em, though."

"Did she ever come back here?"

"No. Years later when she wanted to come home for a visit her papa wouldn't let her. He wouldn't have anything to do with her by that time. They say he even boarded up her room, and that he burned up the portrait he'd had painted of her over in Europe."

"But he didn't burn it up!" cried Randy, and stopped aghast. The blood vow!

"What's that? He didn't? How do you know?"

Just then, thank heaven, Father knocked on the door, and Rush flew to open it.

Randy told Oliver the whole story the next morning. "Just think," she said at the end, "I found the room, I discovered Clarinda in a way, and now it turns out that she wanted to be a great dancer, just like me, and what's more she became one. Why, it's like some kind of magic sign!"

That afternoon they had a meeting in Clarinda's room. Rush presided.

"I think you'll agree," he said, "that the time has come for this place to stop being a secret. Father and Cuffy and Willy and people like Mr. and Mrs. Pepper really have a right to know. What do you think?"

They all agreed wholeheartedly. The secrecy was beginning to weigh on their consciences.

"And besides, now maybe we'll get some real chairs to sit on," observed Oliver realistically from the orange crate. "And Clarinda will have a nice room to live in again."

They all looked at Clarinda, with her rose, her columns, her red dress; and each of them admired her for a different reason.

Mona admired her because she had become famous in spite of everything.

Rush admired her because she had had courage, and because from the beginning she had known and pursued her destiny.

Randy admired her because she had triumphed as a dancer even in that difficult and ancient day.

And Oliver admired her because she had dared to descend from a third-story window on a ladder made entirely out of sheets.

CHAPTER X

The Caddis House

THE remainder of the winter progressed fairly evenly. True, Rush and Randy found it necessary to take some of the starch out of Mona when she referred too loftily to her "program" or her "fan mail." True, too, that Randy's life-and-death struggle with arithmetic never got any easier, and that Rush and Floyd Laramy, though maintaining a sort of armed truce, were never to become bosom friends. True, Oliver had to go to bed without his supper on two unhappy occasions, and Isaac was severely spanked when he eloped with a whole leg of lamb, and all of them got into trouble from time to time: the fact remained that the Melendys always looked back on that winter as one of the pleasantest in their whole lives.

They were so busy. Twice a week Mona and Cuffy departed for New York and Mona's broadcast. Rush gave his lessons every day, and on Sundays the whole family went dutifully to the Methodist church and listened to him play the organ. Randy did a lot of warped-looking knitting and Oliver was building himself a whole fleet of battleships to float in the brook when spring came.

For gradually the winter was beginning to slow down.

The ice thawed, and mud was everywhere. Cuffy had pinned large, stern signs to the back and front doors.

"WIPE YOUR FEET!!" they said. It was still raw and cold, but every now and then there would be a day, or an hour, or a moment, when the sun came out, and there was something different in the air: a sort of glimpsed fragrance, like when the kitchen door is opened for a second while the birthday cake is being baked. It was a smell of promise.

The little brook bellowed hoarsely; there was a swelling at the joints of the twigs, and the first skunk cabbages appeared, brown cowls beside the brook. And at night, tinkling, jingling, gurgling, with high silvery notes, came the voices of the peepers. The dark was spangled with their voices.

Randy and Oliver spent as much time as possible slopping about in the swamp and the brook, or anything else that was sufficiently wet. There were things to find in the water, now that spring was coming. There were frogs' eggs in the swamp pools; great, transparent clumps of tapioca full of black polka dots, each of which would someday be a tadpole and eventually, if all went well, a frog. Randy and Oliver had three jarfuls under observation at home.

In the brook there were caddis houses. Rush had discovered these first. They were tiny cases, not much more than an inch long, and about as big around as a soda straw. They were constructed of bits of twig and shell, tiny pebbles, and choke cherry pits, all held together with a miraculous, silky cement that was created by the retiring little architect who lived inside. All one ever saw of him was a flicker of spidery legs; a tiny, beady head withdrawing.

"Someday he'll come out of there with wings," said Rush, who had looked him up in the dictionary. Randy thought caddis houses were very interesting; she never tired of searching for them, so minute and delicately made, so deceptively like twigs, rolling softly on the floor of the brook.

Out by the stable stood a stricken-looking cage of chicken wire and odd boards. Oliver had built it with time, noise, and effort. "I'm just waiting for the snakes to wake up," he explained. "Then I'm going to catch a few and keep them in here and tame them." Cuffy shuddered at the mere idea, and Mona said, "How revolting!" as usual.

The spring rains were torrential that year. Late in March it rained for three and a half days without stopping: not a pause, not a minute's fitful sunlight; nothing but streaming windows and roaring gutters for three and half solid days. In the morning the Melendys rushed from the front door into the Motor, which smelt terrible in wet weather, and from the Motor they rushed into school. In the afternoon it was the same thing all over again in reverse, from school to Motor; from Motor to house. It was very boring.

However, there were compensations. There was the Office, of course. And above all there was Clarinda's room in which there were now four chairs, a table, and a rag rug; and Clarinda was properly hung ("or do you say hanged, I wonder?" said Rush) on the wall. For the room was no longer a secret. How surprised Father had been! Willy, too, and Cuffy. They had felt a little sheepish, as well, at having overlooked the discrepancy in the Office windows for so long. Everybody came to see it: Mrs. Oliphant all the way from New York; Mr. and Mrs. Wheelwright, the Coughings, the Purvises, old Mr. and Mrs. Pepper, and all their friends at school. Mona had written a theme about it in English class, and the teacher had written "Ex." (which meant excellent) on the upper right-hand corner, and a note which said, "Very orig. subj. well handled." Yes, Clarinda's room was a great success.

The cupola, too, was a good place to be in when it rained. The rain pattered and resounded on the roof; and looking through the four glass windows was like looking through four waterfalls. Randy sat there by the hour (it was too cold for anybody else), humped up in the middle of the cot with an ancient Navajo blanket over her shoulders.

At last, on Saturday afternoon, the rain ceased. Rush closed the lid of his piano and stretched up and up and up as if he would have liked to push his arms right through the roof. "Let's go out, kids, what do you say?"

Randy heard him from the cupola and came tumbling down the ladder-stairs. But Mona didn't want to go out because it was still too wet. She was always like that lately. She seemed to want to do what she thought people ought to want to do. If it was wet, she stayed in; if it was time for bed, she went immediately to bed; if the other girls at school wore ankle socks and pleated skirts, she wore them too: never shorts or overalls. When it was time to do homework, she did homework without dawdling or finding excuses. She never got into trouble of any kind. Of course, she was quite old by now, fourteen, and she was an

acknowledged radio actress, and all that. Still, it was dis-
appointing.

Rush and Randy weren't like that at all. They were
always getting into trouble. They hated going to bed on
time, never desired to do their homework at the appointed
hour, and both wore whatever was handiest, oldest, and
most comfortable. And they both loved wet weather when
it wasn't so violent that it kept them indoors.

"Besides, it isn't really *wet*," Randy insisted. "It's just
dripping a little."

"But it's cold," objected Mona.

"Well, it's the end of March already," said Rush. "It's
not the same kind of cold as winter. And we can wear our
rubber boots."

"Okay," Mona said loftily. "Go on out in it if you
want to, Rush. *I* don't. Get bronchitis again, if you like,
and go around coughing like an old sick mule."

"Oh, nuts," cried Rush. "That was a long time ago.
Christmastime. It sounded worse than it was."

But Randy wasn't going to argue. She didn't enjoy
argument the way Rush did. Already she was rummaging
among the battered piles of foot gear on the closet floor;
among the dozens of rubbers, overshoes, boots, ski boots,
and ice skates that had accumulated there during the past
months.

"Here are your boots, Rush," she said. "But I can only
find one of mine. Mona, can I wear one of yours instead?"

"As far as I'm concerned you can go out barefoot,"
replied Mona haughtily, turning a page of *War and Peace*.
She had taken to reading heavy grown-up books and talk-

ing about them afterward to grownups, who were often impressed.

"The young intellectual," remarked Rush, putting on his old cracked poncho. Randy put on her sticky, yellow slicker, and they went downstairs. When they opened the front door the large, bounding March wind came to greet them. Black, wet branches leaped against the sky, raw and leafless, and shaken drops fell on their heads.

"Listen to the brook!"

It sounded like a river, the brook did, roaring and tumbling between the rocks, swollen and made strong by the rain.

"Where'll we go first, Rush?"

"Up on the hill to see if the tree house blew down."

So they went up the hill through the woods. All about and overhead the wind surged and swam; the branches creaked and scraped and shook cold water down. Below, the soaked, dead leaves of last year clung to their rubber boots.

"Like wet cornflakes," Randy said.

"Like wet corn plasters, you mean," Rush said vulgarly, and they both laughed heartily. It seemed a good joke at the moment. Oh, it was wonderful to be outdoors again.

"Smell how different it is!" cried Randy. "Air never really gets into a house."

It was true. The broad, wild wind had the most wonderful smell; an odor of earth and space and wetness, and the beginnings of spring.

Randy had a little trouble in walking. At every step the Mona rubber boot, which was several sizes too large, kept sinking away from her foot with a hollow, puffing sound. But it wasn't enough to spoil her pleasure.

"Look, it's okay!" said Rush when they came to the top of the hill; and gazing up Randy saw that the tree house was still firmly anchored to the giant branches of the oak. Even though it dipped and swayed, not one board was loose.

"Pretty well constructed," boasted Rush.

"Let's go up!" said Randy. They got the ladder and went up, Rush first, and Randy behind, keeping the Mona boot on by sheer will power and nothing else.

"It's a boat!" she cried when they had clambered over the railing into the tree house. "See how it rocks. You be captain, Rush, and I'll be crew."

"Reef the sail!" ordered Rush, catching on immediately. "A monsoon is coming up. I smell ugly weather in the China Sea."

Randy could smell it too. Excitedly she reefed in imaginary sail while the tree house rolled and tossed: buffeted by wild semitropical tempests.

"A U-boat aft!" shouted Rush. "It's a destroyer now, Randy. Man the guns!" And Randy manned imaginary guns at the top of her lungs.

It was very fine and exciting. When a gathering of crows seesawed windily overhead, cawing in rusty voices, she and Rush let them have imaginary antiaircraft fire. The blood of battle surged in their veins; and soon, though the rusty cawing of the crows continued to clamor faintly on the wind, they were proud victors. About them on the sea the remains of two U-boats and seventeen Japanese fighter planes lay demolished and abandoned.

After a while when they got tired of war, Randy said, "Now let's go and see what the brook's like." As they climbed down the ladder Rush's poncho flapped about his head, and Randy's Mona boot at last fell off, but she found it again.

The brook was even better than they had hoped. At the place where the water habitually came down the rocks in a little waterfall there was now an enormous, brawling cascade, big enough to knock a man off his feet. The banks were submerged, and under the water the little, new, beginning plants and ferns waved frantically to and fro.

They stood and watched the falling water for a long time. There was something magnificent and satisfying in its force and power; when they looked away the land and trees seemed to be moving, too; to be gliding along with the brook. "Sort of like when you're dizzy after rolling downhill," shouted Randy. She had to shout to be heard.

Then they went wading in the comparatively quiet shallows some distance below the fall. The water embraced their rubber boots and inside the boots their toes felt cold but protected. Rush and Randy bent down looking for caddis houses. They invaded a wet, mysterious world. The water was dark and clear, like root beer, and on the bottom they saw shifting sand and pebbles, water-sodden twigs, and glittering flakes of mica. There were lots of caddis houses, and they gathered quite a collection, comparing them and examining the different mosaic patterns of the little tubes.

Suddenly Randy made the strangest sound: a sort of smothered yell.

"What's the matter, Ran?" Rush looked up.

"Oh, oh, *oh!*" was Randy's only reply. She was staring at something in her hand with a flabbergasted expression.

"Well, what *is* it?"

"I think," said Randy slowly. "Rush, I think it's a diamond."

Rush relaxed. "Oh, Randy," he groaned tolerantly. "Wake up. You're always finding diamonds that turn out to be glass, and emeralds that turn out to be pieces of ginger-ale bottle, and gold that's nothing but old beer cans. Don't you ever get discouraged?"

"But look at it, Rush. Please just take a look." She held out her hand. The little case that lay in it was like all the rest: a variation on the same patched-together dwelling place. But there was one difference: halfway down one side of it there was a small, round stone like a tiny glass doorknob. It was no larger than a chokecherry pit, but it was clear as a drop of dew on a fine morning, and its surface was shaped, carved, and faceted in a way that could only have been accomplished by some man's skill.

"Holy Moses," said Rush in a quiet, detached way.

"It is one, isn't it?" said Randy, giving a sort of floundering leap and forgetting about the Mona boot, which instantly fell off and filled with water. She picked it up, tossed it on the bank hardly noticing, and stood like a heron with one wet foot drawn under her.

"Well, I'm not certain," replied Rush, not noticing either. "Of course it's probably only a rhinestone. But even that's queer enough."

"Oh, no, Rush. It's a diamond all right," said Randy with all the assurance of Mr. Tiffany himself. "But what in the world is it doing there, decorating a worm's little house?"

"Darned if I know. Maybe it fell out of a ring or a pin. Maybe years ago, who knows?"

Yes, probably it had fallen out of some lady's ring, and dropped into the water with a tiny splash and disappeared. Randy could see the lady's white hand, long and narrow and snow white, except for pink-polished nails. The hand hovered in and out among violet plants beside the brook. To and fro, and to and fro it went, with the sun striking great shuddering, shifting sparks of light from the diamond on the third finger. Suddenly there is a cry, the violets fall to the earth. "My ring, my ring!" cries the lady's voice. "The stone is gone!"

"I wonder who it belonged to?"

"Chances are you'll never find out. Probably it's only a rhinestone, but you'd better keep it anyway. Here comes Mona, maybe she'll know."

In a half-reluctant, offhand way Mona was coming down to the brook; walking slowly with her galoshes flopping. The thought of outdoors and the wild wind had got between her and the pages of *War and Peace* in spite of her.

"Mona!" cried Randy exultantly. "Guess what! I've just found a diamond stuck to a caddis house!"

"And Willy's struck oil on the front lawn, and Cuffy's inherited a million dollars, and I'm the Countess Natasha Rostova in disguise," replied Mona sarcastically, without altering her pace.

"Well, she's found *something*," said Rush in a solemn, impressive way. "Believe it or not. I think maybe it's the

McCoy this time. Come see." And Mona forgot about her age, talent, and position in the world, and flapped inelegantly across the sodden leaves to the brook.

Randy kept the miraculous caddis case in a tumblerful of water that day and the next; but on Monday she transferred it to a bottle which she put in her schoolbag. During the school lunch hour she bicycled down to see Mr. Lapvogel, the Carthage jeweler.

"Well, I wouldn't of believed it," Mr. Lapvogel said a few minutes later, removing the thimble-shaped magnifier from his eye. "No, sir, I wouldn't of believed it no matter who told me."

"You mean it's really a diamond?"

"The genuwine article. It's a nice little stone: nice color, nice work. Course tisn't big. Couldn't get so much for it."

"About how much would you say, Mr. Lapvogel?"

"For this here? Oh, say around seventy-five, maybe eighty-five."

"Dollars?"

"Sure, dollars. Course you don't want to sell it, though, do you? That's a curiosity, that is. A rare, rare curiosity."

Randy looked down at her jewel with a pang. Probably the only diamond I'll have ever, she thought. The many clocks and little watches in the store ticked and whispered hastily, like insects in old, dry wood. Randy gave a sigh that blew a scrap of paper off the counter.

"No, Mr. Lapvogel. I'm not going to keep it, I'm going to sell it. Everybody in this family has been earning money except me and Oliver; and after all Oliver's only a child of seven. Do you—I mean, would you feel like buying it yourself? You could put it in a ring or something and sell it, couldn't you?"

"Why, sure, guess I could. I'd buy it all right, only don't you think I'd ought to get your papa's permission first? You sure he wants you to sell it?"

Randy said, "Father and I talked it over. He thought you might want to be sure of that so he wrote you a letter. Here it is."

Mr. Lapvogel read the letter and was convinced. "Tell you what, I said seventy-five, maybe eighty-five, didn't I? So I'll give you eighty, that okay?"

"Oh, yes," said Randy faintly. "If you're sure it's not too much."

"Is that any way to close a business deal?" inquired Mr. Lapvogel. "You'd ought to say to me 'Eighty? Well, I don't know. Maybe I better go see what they say over to Braxton,' and like as not I would have offered ninety."

"Oh," said Randy, feeling very young. But Mr. Lapvogel was smiling. He went over to the large, forthright safe at the back of the shop, and squatted down in front of it. Randy watched him twirling the nickel knobs, his brow seamed in concentration, and his lips moving as he recited the combination to himself.

A few minutes later he slammed the safe door shut.

"Seventy. Seventy-five. Eighty," said Mr. Lapvogel, counting out the soft, old bills. "There 'tis." Randy had never seen so much money in her life. She folded it respectfully, and stuffed it, bulging, into her patent leather pocketbook.

"I'm going to put your diamond on display in my window," said Mr. Lapvogel. "Right slam in the middle of the window on a kind of black velvet stand, with a card attached telling the whole story."

"I'll come and look at it often, with a covetous eye," said Randy. She could imagine her diamond, throned on velvet; the center, the climax, of Mr. Lapvogel's distinguished, though flyspecked, collection: a costly display of enamel lockets and novelty pins shaped like everything from an elephant to Mickey Mouse; link bracelets, wrist watches, bead necklaces, engagement rings, and at the back an arrangement of electric clocks looking on gravely, like a jury.

"And I'm going to tell Cal Joiner about it first. He's editor down to the *Post-Clarion*. He'll put a piece about it in the paper, with your name and all. Maybe your photo too."

There was a certain satisfaction in that idea. Randy paused at the doorway. "I'm kind of scared to walk down the street," she confided. "I never felt so valuable before."

"What you going to do with all that cash?" inquired Mr. Lapvogel. "Buy a little fur coat?"

"No, indeed." Randy looked at him proudly. "I'm going to buy a War Bond. Mona's bought two out of her own earnings, and Rush has one out of his, and there's another that belongs to all of us together from our show. But I'm going to get this one by myself with my diamond money."

"Well, you're a patriotic girl and a good citizen," said Mr. Lapvogel approvingly. "Maybe I'd ought to of given you ninety after all."

Randy laughed at him and waved her pocketbook. "Is that any way to close a business deal?" she said.

The little Carthage bank lay at the foot of the hill beside the church. She had been there with Father several times and knew Mr. Craven quite well. He was a tall grey man with glasses who always peered through the bars of his cage and said, "My, my, almost as tall as Daddy, aren't you? When are you going to open a checking account with us?" Then he would give a little dry laugh like the crackle of a new dollar bill.

"How do you do, Mr. Craven," said Randy, with dignity. "I would like to buy a bond. A War Bond."

"Don't you mean a stamp, sister?" said Mr. Craven, glancing at her in a grown-up way.

She opened her purse and spilled the money out on the shelf in front of his cage. "I want as big a bond as that can buy. And here's a note from my father telling you it's all right."

Mr. Craven's eyes widened. He looked as if he would like to know where she had got all those bills. Randy didn't tell him, though she would have enjoyed watching his face if she had said, "You see, Mr. Craven, I found this diamond in our brook the other day—"

The bond was a fine one; substantial and important looking; and there was even some money left over. Not much, but enough so that after school Randy was able to go and buy presents for her family. She rode home on her bicycle, after a glorious hour of shopping, with the wire carrier full of presents, and the bond pinned with a large safety pin to the inside of her blouse. It had a starchy tickle against her ribs, but she didn't mind.

The sky was warm and blue; a robin flew across the

road, and there were tassels on the alders. The forsythia bushes were almost in bloom: they rested light, golden, frothy, like sunlit clouds along the fences. Randy sang as she rode; she had not yet recovered from her good fortune. Why, it's a miracle, she kept thinking, I had a real honest-to-goodness miracle happen to me. Whoever heard of a girl just putting her hand into a brook and picking up a diamond? But it happened; and to me! That's the thing I can't get over.

She coasted on the long downhill part of the drive, and coasting, stared at the scene before her: she saw it very sharp and clear. The funny, fancy old house, and the towering, somber spruce trees, and the scattered crows that seemed always to be hovering and calling high above.

Rush and Isaac were running out of the woods, with Isaac barking; Oliver was sitting astride one of the iron deer, wearing a cowboy hat and all his MacArthur buttons; Cuffy and Mona were bent over a flower bed examining the new rabbit-ears of green that sprouted from the damp earth. Father's absorbed profile could be seen in the study window, and Willy, wearing faded blue overalls, was burning off the dead grass on the lawn. The air smelled deliciously of smoke.

Randy swooped expertly around the driveway circle, brought her bike to a slow and graceful stop and dismounted. As she gathered up her presents from the wire carrier, the bond crackled against her chest. Yes, finding the diamond had been a miracle. But Randy couldn't help feeling that there were many miracles in her life. Wasn't it a miracle to live in the country in spring? And to have a wonderful family that she was crazy about, and a house with a secret room and a cupola, and to be eleven and a half years old, and very good at riding a bicycle?

Anyway that's how I feel today, thought Randy. Tomorrow maybe I'll feel some other way; cranky, or dull, or just natural. But that's how I feel today.

CHAPTER XI

Addition and Subtraction

AND at last it was really spring: flowers everywhere.
The woods were carpeted with them: bloodroot
wrapped in its cloak like an Indian princess, trillium, jack-
in-the-pulpit, Dutchman's-breeches, hepatica (blooming
out of a little fur mitten) and dogtooth violet. Down near
the creek there were real violets by the hundred, by the
thousand, starring their heartshaped leaves. Even the trees
were full of flowers, apple blossom, and snowy pear, and
cherry. Of two huge lopsided bushes near the house, one
suddenly burst into a rash of orange rosettes and the other
turned into a shower of pink fringe almost overnight.

Each day the children woke early and couldn't bear
not to get up. The birds made such a racket: such a
warbling and calling and whistling and rustling in the
trees and vines; and the smell that drifted in through the
open windows was so wildly exciting; a fragrance so new,
never breathed before, so sweet and mysterious and in-
viting that one couldn't stay indoors, much less in bed.
Cuffy was constantly having to put her head out the window to tell people to come in "and put on some bedroom
slippers at *least!*"

On Saturdays and Sundays life was pleasantly disorganized; nobody had meals in the house. They wandered about, eating sandwiches in the woods, in the orchard, beside the brook, anywhere. The brook was a never-failing source of delight. Rush invented a sport called "sure-footing" which consisted of leaping with speed, agility, and daring from boulder to half-submerged boulder. As a result, there was always a pair of sneakers out drying on somebody's window sill at the Four-Story Mistake, and there were frequently shorts, shirts, and dresses on the clothesline as well. Usually Randy's shorts and dresses: she fell in oftenest.

Rush and Willy started an ambitious Victory Garden, and Mona and Cuffy and Randy took care of the flower garden. Oliver veered between one and the other as his fancy took him, and sometimes (quite often) he just forgot about them both. The world seemed to expand with spring. It was larger, newer. The woods became thick and deep; and familiar vistas were hidden, made secret by thousands and thousands of opening leaves. Grass rose up tall and soft on the fields like fur on the back of a cat. Everything had to be explored all over again, for suddenly all had been created anew.

Many interesting things happened to the Melendys that spring. Many additions were made to the household. For one thing, another dog came to live with them. On a sunny day in late April a ragged, jet-black mongrel appeared from nowhere and never left again. Nobody had ever seen or heard of the dog before; he simply materialized, appeared, and became their devoted companion from then onward. They called him John Doe,

Johnny for short, and he and Isaac were a happy pair, hunting for the same rabbits, collecting similar burrs and ticks, and at night lying side by side, paws twitching, noses quivering, as apparently they dreamed the same dreams.

They got a goat, too. Her name was Persephone and they called her Phoney for short. She was a snow-white nanny goat with long, wicked yellow eyes that belied her gentle, almost sentimental nature. Mona and Randy learned how to milk her, and felt like Heidi every time they drank the chalk-white milk. Phoney was a darling: they all loved her, even though she did eat up half the paper salvage one day, and a part of the metal salvage the next.

Oliver and Rush collected snakes. It was no trick at all to catch them now, for the snakes were still drowsy and slow from their long winter sleep and lay idly among the old leaves in the woods. They had two handsome king snakes named King Cole and King Kong, and a black one called Licorice. Licorice was Oliver's favorite, and accompanied him about the place wrapped around his arm or his middle, to Cuffy's horror and disgust.

"Not in the house, you don't!" cried Cuffy. "Never in the house. One alligator is all the reptiles we can handle in the house, and by the way, Willy, isn't it time you brought Crusty's tank outdoor? It's warm enough now."

So Crusty, who had grown fat on a diet of canned fish, chop bones, and hamburger, was brought outdoors to lie in his own private swimming bath on the back lawn. The birds came to look at him curiously, and he looked back at them still as a log, smiling disarmingly, and daring them to come closer.

The newest and one of the best additions to their family arrived late in May.

One Sunday afternoon, tiring of his typewriter, Father went to the kitchen and opened the icebox door. There he saw part of a leg of lamb, and thought to himself "Cold lamb sandwiches with horseradish." Then he closed the door and thought "Why not a picnic?"

So that is how it happened. In less than an hour they had all, including Isaac and John Doe, piled into the Motor. It was a heavenly day. The leaves burned with that pure-green light that is seen only in spring, and there were daisies and buttercups all along the roadside.

"Never plan a picnic," Father said. "Plan a dinner, yes, or a house, or a budget, or an appointment with the dentist, but never, never plan a picnic."

They all agreed with him: it was so pleasant to find themselves setting out with sandwiches made of this and that, to a destination which might be here or there.

"We may find an oasis with coconut palms, or a snow-capped peak, or a crater lake," suggested Father. "We'll stop at the first place that takes our eye."

But Fate, who was hovering by and cackling maliciously, chose to strike then and there on a back road three miles from home. The Motor suddenly lurched, stumbled, and waddled a short distance before Willy stopped it.

"Tire?" said Father.

"Tire," replied Willy.

"Where's the spare?"

"That was the spare," said Willy sorrowfully.

It was a bitter blow. Now, when tires were as hard to get as crowns of gold.

"Farewell to the oasis of palms," sighed Father. "And farewell to the snow-capped peak. I guess we'll have to eat our supper over in that cow pasture, after all."

But it tasted just as good in the cow pasture. And besides there was a fine brook there, all lined with watercress, which was a pleasant surprise.

Cuffy's picnics were very complete affairs, because along with the sandwiches and cooky box there was always a box of band-aids, and cheek-by-jowl with the bottle of horseradish there were always the bottles of citronella and iodine. "For a new taste sensation try a cold lamb sandwich with citronella," Father said. "Or a dash of iodine is very interesting with peanut butter."

At six o'clock they trudged homewards along the dusty road. Sometimes the dogs were running far ahead of them, and sometimes they were dawdling far behind, sniffing at hedges, but they hardly ever stayed beside them. Cuffy puffed along majestically, carrying cress done up in a handkerchief. Father was walking with a tall stick, like Tannhäuser, and talking to Willy in a low voice; whenever anyone came near he waved the stick at them, and told them to beat it. Between Rush and Mona the empty picnic basket knocked from side to side; and Oliver and Randy skipped, ran, sidled, hopped, climbed fences, balanced on rails, but never merely walked.

Far behind them the Motor leaned to one side, old, tired, and alone.

After that the Melendys rode to school on their bicycles, and Willy, to the astonishment and intense joy of the children, the village of Carthage, and in fact the entire county, refurbished the giant wheeled antique from Oliver's cellar room, and on it creaked, wobblingly, about the country-side like a mechanized Ichabod Crane.

But the tenth day after the disablement of the Motor the children returned from school to find Father and Willy out in front of the house waiting for them.

"Hello, kids," called Father, and there was a certain jubilant quality in his voice. "We've got a surprise for you."

"A surprise? Where is it?" cried Oliver, leaping from his bike.

"In the stable," said Father, as they followed him along at a brisk clip. Could it be something alive?

Looking in they saw the Motor, propped up on a jack for the duration. And beside the Motor there was an old-fashioned surrey with a fringed roof, and in the first stall there was a horse.

A horse!

"Now the stable is really a stable," said Oliver in the quiet voice of great happiness.

"And it's a dapple grey," cried Mona. "My favorite color of horse!"

Already Randy was reaching up to pat the silky, dewy muzzle, and Rush had climbed the wooden wall in order to get a better view.

"Where did you ever get it, father?"

"Up the valley from a farmer named Peterson."

"What's the horse's name?"

"Lorna Doone. She's a mare."

"And someday can she have a colt?"

"There goes Oliver living in the future again," said Father, laughing. "Maybe she'll have a colt someday, and maybe she won't. But what's the matter with her as she is?"

There was nothing the matter with her. Willy showed Rush how to harness her to the surrey and they all took a ride. The fringes waved festively and Willy drove as though he had been a coachman all his life.

"It's so much better than the Motor," Randy said, "because all you could smell in the Motor was gas fumes and old imitation leather. This way you get the benefit of the air and the flowers and grass with a nice smell of horse added."

"Now we have eight animals," mused Oliver, taking inventory. "A horse, a goat, two dogs, three snakes, and an alligator. But don't you think we ought to have a cow and a pig and some chickens, father?"

"Yes now that you mention it I do. And a kiwi bird, and a laughing hyena, and a three-toed sloth."

"Do you really mean it?" Oliver's face was a blaze of hope. "And next winter will the horse pull us to school in a sleigh?"

Early in June they had the first thunderstorm. It came after a hot, satisfactory day that had included a ride in the surrey and a picnic supper. It came, also, as storms so often do, in the middle of the night. In the eastern sky a distant growling had been going on for some time, but everybody in the Four-Story Mistake was fast asleep: they knew nothing about it until it arrived full force with the thunder booming and splitting, the rain beating down in steady hammers, and the lightning coming and going as swiftly and frequently as the flickering of a snake's tongue.

"Great day!" cried Cuffy, springing out of bed and

reaching for her kimono with one hand and the light switch with the other. But the lights were out again (of course) and she had to go padding about with a candle, closing windows and wiping up puddles. Father got up, too, and after a while the whole family, except Oliver who slept through it, was twinkling about the house with flashlights.

"Ouch!" Randy would exclaim every time there was a particularly deafening crash. Then she would smile unconvincingly and say, "I think I'm getting so I kind of like thunderstorms." But nobody was fooled.

Rush really did like them, and this was a good one. He stood looking out the window. During the frequent flashes he could see wildly tossing trees frozen for an instant in uncanny light. He could see the white, blank puddles staring back at the sky, and torn leaves driven through the air, and the iron deer bravely indifferent to it all: one standing proud and imperious, staring into space, the other forever grazing with a meek and downward neck.

"Get back to bed, now, get back to bed," commanded Cuffy. "My lands, the peonies will be beaten to a pulp after this, I'm afraid. All right, Randy, you can come and sleep in my room if you want to. Only remember, *no talking!*"

It rained so hard that night that the brook again swelled its boundaries, and as Cuffy had predicted, the peonies were beaten down and completed their blooming in a supine position on the grass. It rained so hard that poor, forgotten Crusty's tank filled up to the brim and overflowed, and Crusty, seeing his chance, swam up to the edge and overflowed with it.

Flapping his tail, and stretching his short ugly legs, the alligator savored freedom and took his bearings. Ah, water! The smell of water! Not rain water, not tank water, but live water, going somewhere! Slowly, clumsily, but with something like a sense of adventure quickening his thick blood, Crusty crawled toward the brook, grinning from ear to ear.

At breakfast the next day Willy burst into the dining room.

"Say, Mr. Melendy! That alligator! He's gone, got out, beat it! I can't find him nowheres. Musta scrammed last night when the rain filled up his tank."

"Gone?" cried Oliver and Rush and Randy in voices of consternation. "Gone?" cried Father and Mona in blank surprise.

But Cuffy said, "You mean he's honestly gone?" and on her face there was unmistakable relief.

"It's going to be very hard for me to believe that Mrs. Cuthbert-Stanley didn't have something to do with this. Did you, Cuffy?" said Father. They all turned to look at Cuffy, who, stainless of guilt though she was, blushed right up to the roots of her white hair.

They never saw Crusty again. They searched, advertised, warned the farmers in the valley, but never a trace of Crusty did they find. Two years later Father, returning from a lecture in Philadelphia, brought them a small clipping from a newspaper which was headed:

SEEING THINGS?

Natives of Humboldt Quarter, Pa., have recently reported the presence of a live alligator in Humboldt Creek. Five people claim to have seen it, the last being Herman C. Rollstoner, local butcher, who says he saw it Sunday, while fishing. Rollstoner took the pledge on Monday. Authorities claim it extremely unlikely that an alligator of the size reported (about two and a half feet) could survive in such northerly waters.

"Do you suppose it could be Crusty?" cried Randy.

"Could be," Rush said. "The authorities probably never saw an alligator with such a determined character."

CHAPTER XII

"Oh, Summer Night!"

MONA was going to a dance. A real dance at school: a Boy was taking her. No Melendy child had ever done such a thing before.

Randy sat on the foot of her sister's bed watching her get ready.

"I don't see what you want to go for," she said, "and with that old Chris Cottrell, too."

"He's all right," replied Mona from her new adult altitude, and then descended from it to say anxiously, "Oh dear, I hope I don't step on his feet. Do you think I will?"

"You won't be able to miss them, they're as big as a couple of cellos," said Randy crossly.

"I'm kind of scared," confided Mona. But when she slipped the dress over her head, the new dress that she and Cuffy had made, the annoyingly distant composure returned to her face.

The dress was pretty. It had a long, full skirt, really long, right down to the floor; and it was made out of thin pink cotton stuff, nineteen cents a yard at the Carthage Dry Goods and Confectionery.

"Jeepers, you look old," commented Rush, looking in at the door, "about eighteen or nineteen at least."

"Do I really, Rush?" Mona was delighted.

"Yep. But I don't see why you want to."

"I'm tired of looking callow. Listen, kids, shall I wear these roses on top of my head, or sort of on the side by the parting?"

"Oh, wear them between your teeth like Carmen," said Rush, wheeling away from the door. "I think you're getting kind of silly, Mona."

Mona didn't care. Her eyes were shining, her cheeks pink, as they always were when she was excited. The roses in her hair were very becoming. Randy sighed, and watched her gloomily.

"Gee whiz, you're getting so grown up. Pretty soon you won't be any fun at all."

"Don't be silly. There's the doorbell!" Mona gave her a kiss without thinking about her, snatched up her summer coat and hurried down to the living room where Chris and her father were talking to Cuffy.

After they had gone Randy went slowly up the stairs to the Office. She felt awful. Rush was at the piano practicing the first of the Brahms-Handel Variations. "When I'm about twenty-one I ought to be able to do 'em pretty well if I start now and work hard," he'd said.

Randy sat first in one chair and then in another. She tiptoed into Clarinda's room and back again, took a book out of the bookcase and replaced it; stared at one of the newspaper pictures on the wall; tiptoed up to the cupola, looked out at the moonlit world without seeing it, and then tiptoed down again. Finally she sat down in a creaky wicker chair and sighed deeply.

"Say, what's the matter with you anyway?" asked Rush, turning from his music. "You've been circulating around here like a draft."

"I don't know what's the matter with me," Randy said mournfully. "I guess it's that I hate having any of us grow up."

"But we're not grown up," Rush observed briskly. "None of us. Not even Mona."

"She almost is. Dances, radio acting, and all that. She even puts powder on her nose sometimes."

Rush flipped the pages of his music. "What do you care? I'm still here."

"You won't be long. Pretty soon you'll start going to dances yourself. With girls and things."

"For Pete's sake, Ran. You know how I hate all that stuff."

"You will, though," persisted Randy, a soothsayer disliking her wisdom. "Pretty soon you'll always be slicking down your hair, and talking hours and hours on the telephone, and cleaning your fingernails without being told."

"Oh, shut up. I will not."

"Yes, you will. And you'll be careful of your clothes, and always play lovey-dovey music on the piano—"

But that was too much. With a yelp of rage Rush leaped from the piano bench and chased Randy, shrieking and laughing, all the way downstairs and out of doors before he caught her.

"I take it back, I take it back," squeaked Randy in a cowardly way; and Rush released her.

Oliver was standing in the doorway wearing pajamas with blue Dumbos all over them.

"What was the running and the noise about?"

"Rush and I had an argument, that's all," said Randy, hugging him in spite of his protests. "Oliver darling, I'm so glad you're only seven!"

When Mona came home at half past ten she found Randy waiting up for her. Or rather she found Randy asleep in her bed, with the lights on, and a note pinned to the sheet under her chin which said, "Wake me up and talk."

"Wake up, wake up," called Mona in a whisper, shaking her sister's shoulder; and Randy grumbled, protested, and finally pulled herself together and sat up.

Mona was wearing her dressing gown. The pink dress lay in a crumpled wreath on the floor, and she was pulling off her slippers impatiently.

"Ooh, my feet, my feet."

"Did you have a good time?"

"Oh, yes, wonderful. Everybody danced with me, even Mr. Coughing. I didn't step on anybody's toes either, but lots of people stepped on mine."

"Are you glad you went?"

"Yes, it was an Experience. But I think I'll enjoy it more when I'm older. You know, sophisticated, with a permanent wave and all."

Mona wiggled her bare toes luxuriously.

"Let's go out, it's a wonderful night, and I'm going to bathe my feet in the brook, they're so hot and stepped-on. Let's get Rush too. Oliver would only be walking in his sleep, so we won't bother *him*."

Rush awoke with the alacrity of one to whom sleep is a tedious waste of time. "Let's go out via the kitchen," he suggested.

Quietly, quietly they went down the stairs. For some reason they had all begun to laugh, and every now and then it was necessary to pause, holding back the wild laughter that struggled inside them, hugging their ribs, aching with it. It escaped only in short, stifled gusts, and hiccups. None of them could have told you what they were laughing at.

Recovered, but still gasping, they achieved the kitchen where there was so much moonlight streaming in through the screen door that they didn't have to turn on the light to find the cooky jar and the root beer.

"Don't let it slam," cautioned Mona, arms full, holding the door open with her heel.

Beside the house the white peonies looked huge and pearly, shining out of their dark leaves. The air was full of their clean-clothes fragrance; and the honeysuckle was beginning; you knew it every time you took a breath.

Like ghosts the children walked across the lawn on their bare feet. The moon was full. Above the damp grass hung a veil of mist, luminous with moonlight and spangled with fireflies. There was no wind, and the sound of the brook was very distinct, tinkling, splashing, rushing softly. It made Mona think of an ancient fountain, shaped like a shell, covered with moss, and set in a secluded garden: something she half remembered, or imagined.

"How warm it is," cried Randy, suddenly leaping and pirouetting across the dewy grass. "Oh, summer, summer, summer!"

A rank smell of fresh water and soaked maple keys came upward from the brook as they approached. It lay concealed, deep in inky shadow, with only an occasional glimmer of light wavering on its surface.

"Gosh!" said Rush appreciatively. "Imagine sleeping when you can be out in this!"

They walked carefully in the darkness, trying to avoid the places where they remembered rocks or poison ivy, and finally they came to the little pool above the falls. Rush put the root-beer bottles in the water to cool.

Mona felt that the moment called for a suitable quotation and thought of one after a brief scramble through her mind. She began it in a low hushed voice.

"How sweet the moonlight sleeps upon this bank!
Here we will sit—"

"And bathe our aching feet," said Rush, quickly nipping her in the bud. "Listen, Mona, we know you know ten city blocks of quotations from Shakespeare."

"All right," said Mona good-naturedly, and they sat down side by side on a rock with their feet in the dark cool water. After a while when it was cold enough they drank the root beer and ate the cookies. Occasionally they slapped at mosquitoes, but without these tiny flaws the hour would have been too perfect.

Against the shadows fireflies wrote their meaningless hieroglyphics. Rush caught one and held it gently in his closed hand, watching the cold light come and go, come and go, between his fingers.

"This is better than the city," he said.

"Better than the other valley, or the lighthouse even," said Randy.

WITH THEIR FEET IN THE DARK COOL WATER

"Better than anywhere we ever lived," said Mona.

From under the canopy of leaves they looked across the lawn to the big, square house, blue-white in the moonlight. Its windows were black, and so were the sharp shadows under its eaves, and the heavy fringes of the spruce trees which swept the roof. They thought it looked very beautiful.

At last Randy stood up with a little splash. "I'm going to bed and write a poem," she said.

"I've got some music beginning in my head right now that may be good enough for Opus III," Rush announced, and Mona said that she planned to go back to her room and recite all the Shakespeare she wanted, far from the sensitive ears of her brother.

But as it happened the poem never got beyond a single opening phrase: "Oh, summer night!" The music for Opus III was completed only in a dream; and as for the quotations from Shakespeare, that evening, at least, they never were recited at all.

Out of doors the night lived out its life serenely and splendidly. Toward morning a small wind began to blow, as though it came from far, far away; as though it were the first ripple of an advancing tide. With its coming the night commenced to dissolve, to weaken, and though one could see no daylight yet, a rooster miles away knew better, and began to crow.

And now the birds were waking up: at first only one, with a drowsy, broken chirp, and then another and another till the air was spattered with a thousand different notes.

At a quarter to seven Cuffy opened the kitchen door and

out flew Isaac and John Doe, running madly, careening in circles, flinging themselves upon the grass with their eyes rolling, like prisoners who had been pent up for a lifetime. A smell of coffee mingled with the honeysuckle.

At half past seven Cuffy herself came out, breathing the morning air and bending over to see how the rose moss was coming along. Funny none of the children are awake yet, thought Cuffy, straightening and looking up at the quiet windows. Well, school is over, summer is just beginning, and they are children. Let them sleep a little longer. Let them sleep.